PRAISE FOR THE SMART MONEY WOMAN

A practical, no-holds-barred guide to building wealth for the 21st century African woman. Written in an engaging style and full of actionable strategies, this money book is a must-have for every bookshelf.
Aisha Ahmad
Chairperson, WIMBIZ & Head, Consumer Banking & Wealth, Diamond Bank

A journey through personal finance written from a truly African context by a gifted young woman who seeks to reposition and redefine the way we think about the subject.
Aigboje Aig-Imoukhuede, CON,
President, The Nigerian Stock Exchange

There can't be any question whether the concept of finance is important for every woman, and this book brings it to life. Arese provides insights, real-world examples and practical advice about the importance of getting it right. She has again showed us money is a partner in a relationship that must thrive for us to enjoy! Completely educative, easy to read, and most enjoyable.
Osayi Alile
Head, ACT Foundation

Unprecedented. A Nigerian woman's answer to 'Rich Dad, Poor Dad'. Using prose and a mirror, Arese demystifies the art of money making by analysing and conquering the African woman's fear of investments. She tackles the financial taboos and shackling mindsets using our everyday realities to connect. A must read!
Bolanle Austen-Peters
Producer, Director, & Founder, Terra Kulture & BAP Productions

An entertaining way to learn about money... ushering in a new narrative of Africa, specifically of the African woman in the 21st century—her perspective, her ambitions, her journey, flaws and all, but wholly hers.
Alhaji Aliko Dangote, GCON,
Chairman & CEO, Dangote Group

Great storytelling with a strong message and focus on changing or improving your view on money matters. You have a good laugh, set in a familiar place, and most of all you close the book determined to change your money habits.
Tara Fela-Durotoye
Founder, House of Tara

A must-read for anyone looking to have a better understanding of financial literacy. Arese provides a straight-talking, practical, step-by-step approach to a better financial future. A great self-help guide for the young, driven, entrepreneurial African woman.
Peace Hyde
Correspondent, Forbes Africa

Arese puts an interesting and picturesque spin on how women can better manage her money in the book 'The Smart Money Woman'. She addresses the issue of money management in a way every woman can relate to. The style is mellifluous yet profound in its message.
Betty Irabor
Publisher, Genevieve Magazine

Arese wraps fundamental truths in humour and real life relatable experiences, impacting knowledge and a guide to making better choices financially. Such a breath of fresh air for the 21st century woman on her way to financial freedom.
Toke Makinwa
Celebrity & Media Entrepreneur

Money is a hard topic to think and talk about, but Arese breaks it down and removes the fear and discomfort for young African women.
Afua Osei
Co-Founder, She Leads Africa

'The Smart Money Woman' is the modern African woman's book and Zuri's captivating story will keep you turning the page. The real kicker comes in the Smart Money Lessons included in every chapter; easily digestible but vital lessons on how to get started up the financial success ladder. You get double the value with this book—an entertaining read and a valuable education. Well done, Arese.
Uche Pedro
Founder, BellaNaija

THE SMART MONEY WOMAN

An African Girl's Journey to Financial Freedom

ARESE UGWU

Copyright © 2016 Arese Ugwu
First Published by Smart Media Africa

Published by:
Smart Media Africa
info@smartmoneyafrica.org
www.smartmoneyafrica.org
Instagram: @smartmoneyarese
Twitter:@smartmoneyarese
Facebook: www.facebook.com/smartmoneywitharese

All rights reserved. No part of this publication may be reproduced, stored in any retrieval system or transmitted in any form or by any methods, electronic, mechanical, photocopying, recording, or otherwise without the written permission of the publisher.

Package of Edition
ISBN 978-978-955-046-3

Cover Illustration: Peniel Enchill
Design: Yetunde Shorters
Photography: TY Bello

For my daughter Zikora.
I hope this inspires you to live life fearlessly.

ACKNOWLEDGEMENTS

I'm officially an author guys! This journey has been unreal and there are a number of people I would like to thank because I couldn't have done it without them.

My parents, who taught me early on to be fearless in the pursuit of my dreams. My dad, who started talking to me about the capital markets from the age of seven. My mum who taught me the value of money and made me track my expenses every term and threatened not to give me pocket money if I didn't. Thank you!

My siblings Isoken, Kolapo and Ivie who are absolute rock stars! You took the time to read all the different versions of this book and were my first set of critics and encouragers. I love you.

My BFFs Nadine Domingo, Nnenna Okoye, Mariah Lucciano-Gabriel, Toke Makinwa and Eniola Taiwo. You all listened to me go on and about the characters in the book like they were our friends in real life and allowed me to test out dialogue. I love you guys. Thank you for your patience and support.

To my mentors, Bolanle Austen-Peters, Tara Fela Durotoye and Osayi Alile, who have all taught me that no goal is too big, continuously challenge me to set new goals and smash them. Your investment in me can never be repaid. I am extremely grateful.

To my boy besties: Cyril Akpofure who has been on this Smart Money journey with me since day zero and has been the technological backbone of this entire operation. I couldn't have done this without you. To Tobi Osoba who, when I thought I couldn't do this, supported me through my many meltdowns. You are awesome.

To Fela Durotoye who despite his extremely busy schedule would talk to me for two hours at a time on the phone when I got stuck. I am blessed to have you in my life. To Steve Harris, Mr Ruthless Execution; we both know this book would have never happened if you didn't keep me accountable, so thank you for sticking with me even when I was running away. I'm extremely grateful.

To Nimi Akinkugbe, who graciously agreed to write the foreword for this book, took the time to read every chapter and give me her notes even when she was on holiday in St. Lucia and I was stalking her. Thank you so much.

To My editor Tolu Orekoya, who came on board at the tail end but has had a huge impact and made this book so much stronger. It was a gruelling process, the discourse, the early mornings, the late nights, the disagreements over character development, the way you fell in love with the characters combined with your commitment to the work inspires me greatly. Just know you'll never be able to get rid of me. You have a friend for life. I will always be grateful to Chude for introducing us.

To my lawyer and friend Mikki a.k.a. Nneoma Okoli who had to deal with all my ridiculous timelines. God bless you.

To my assistant Temi, who has worked with me for only six months but has been there through all the behind the scenes struggles. I appreciate you.

To My WIMBIZ family! WIMBIZ raised me! Thank you for creating a sustainable platform that empowers and facilitates opportunities for young women like me.

To all the people who lent me their platforms even before I even knew what Smart Money was going to be and helped me find my voice. BellaNaija, Genevieve magazine, the Guardian, Ndani TV and YNaija. Thank you.

To members of the Smart Money movement, your quest to learn more about personal finance, your questions, your emails, your comments on social media, Instagram especially informed a lot of the solutions in this book. I am humbled by your constant support

To my daughter Zikora, who had to contend with the fact that this Smart Money movement is my second child and her baby sister. Instead of getting jealous, she would tease me by calling me "Smart Money" then tell me she wants to be like me when she grows up. I love you baby. I do this for you.

To God almighty for giving me this gift and helping me complete this book despite all the obstacles that were thrown my way. Baba God I thank You.

FOREWORD

When Arese invited me to write the foreword for her first book, 'The Smart Money Woman', I did not hesitate for one minute. Having observed her money ministry through her Smart Money blog, news articles, and television shows, I applaud the huge impact that she is having on the African woman and beyond. It is therefore a real delight to welcome this unique addition to the world of personal finance.

'The Smart Money Woman' is a charming piece of work that will educate those that care to take concrete steps to change their financial lives. This book offers the unique combination of a light-hearted fictional novel in Arese's compelling and engaging style, filled with familiar, vivid characters, accompanied by serious underlying Smart Money Lessons—a beginner's guide to managing her personal finance.

For many people the subject of personal financial management can be somewhat daunting. The book presents the basic concepts of earning, budgeting, spending, borrowing, saving, investing as well as the behavioural and emotional aspects of money in a practical way that makes it easy to personalise.

In the narrative, Arese perfectly captures the picture of a young Nigerian woman, Zuri, whose intellect, educational background, and looks have presented her with great prospects; yet she comes close to losing it all before the realisation that her lifestyle could destroy those same prospects. Whilst the main focus is on Zuri and her journey to financial awakening, the rich characterisation of other primary actors woven through the tale makes it a must read.

Arese's strong background in wealth management more than

qualifies her to present this treasure trove of Smart Money Lessons. She is a role model who demonstrates her teachings; if you imbibe sound financial habits in your youth, with consistent hard work, and a dedicated savings and investment plan, you can build a life of long-term financial security and enjoy a lifestyle of comfort and dignity.

The underlying message in 'The Smart Money Woman' is a positive one; with determination, commitment and time, you can transform your financial life. "Building wealth is more about how much you keep, not about how much you spend," she writes in the book; it is the habit, the discipline of setting something aside regularly to meet your financial goals.

Having observed the money personality of people of substantial means over close to three decades, I have come to the conclusion that there is a discipline associated with creating, building, retaining and transmitting wealth. Those who really seek to accumulate wealth and pass it on in a structured way, do so by setting clear goals and then by consistent saving and long term investing in a diversified asset portfolio towards achieving them. They also maintain a frugal mind set and a cautious approach to spending. They *do* look for bargains, they *do* buy assets on sale and look for discounts, they *do* vet the restaurant bill, and they *do* plan ahead for major spending; and most of all, they do not waste money. Acquiring and maintaining long-term wealth is a process. There usually are no short cuts, but the rewards over time, are well beyond the thrills of instant gratification.

If you are looking for a book that succeeds in unravelling the often perplexing and complex world of money management in the form of a novel, then Arese Ugwu's 'The Smart Money Woman' is for you. An engaging read, it brings the subject of personal finance to life. This book is for every woman; married, single, divorced, widowed; and for every man with women in their lives.

Nimi Akinkugbe
CEO Bestman Games,
Money Matters with Nimi
Lagos, Nigeria
June 2016

TABLE OF CONTENTS

Acknowledgments...vii

Foreword..xi

Broke..1

Money Fears..16

Where Is Your Money Going?.............................32

Dealing With Debt...56

Surviving Emergencies...69

Money Goals...81

The Spending Plan..100

The Power Of Networking.................................117

Life Happens...136

The Long Game..152

Earning More..179

Becoming A Smart Money Woman.................204

CHAPTER 1
BROKE...

I can't believe this is happening to me! Zuri panicked as she shook her head and stared at her account balance. It was the middle of the month and she had a little over eighty thousand left in her bank. To be fair, this would seem like a lot to some, but her expenses told a different story. This balance would barely make a dent in the bills she had piled up, and she wasn't expecting any new funds till the end of the month. Even then, she wouldn't be able to cover the bills that had just arrived.

She stared hopelessly at the papers in front of her. A bill from her mechanic for what she thought were minor repairs had ballooned to two hundred thousand. Her car was now stuck at his workshop until she was able to make payment. There was a letter from her landlord pointing out her service charge bills for the last three months—four hundred and thirty thousand naira in total—were unpaid, and he was threatening to cut her off if payment wasn't made by the end of the month. She had just visited her gynaecologist for a routine check-up, only to discover that she had fibroids. The procedure Dr Emeka had told her she might need would cost nine hundred and fifty thousand, and her HMO had just written to inform her that her plan did not cover it. Dr Emeka was the best, and sometimes the best cost a lot.

She did the math and it didn't add up. She earned six hundred thousand a month after taxes from her job as a senior manager at Richmond Developments, a real estate firm. Until this moment, she had considered herself very lucky. She had a great job that paid well. She lived in an upmarket part of Lagos in Lekki Phase I, in a two-bedroom serviced apartment that overlooked the water. She drove a second-hand Mercedes ML 500, and it was awesome—until the engine started acting up. She could take one or two trips abroad a year to destinations like Dubai, New York or London. To her, that was the ideal life of a single, über-successful twenty-eight-year-old African woman.

So how could she explain to anyone that she was flat broke?

She still couldn't understand it herself. She wasn't overly extravagant. Yes, she liked the good life, but she wouldn't consider herself one of those people living beyond their means. In fact, she hated that term. She could just hear Aunty Iyabo's voice in her head saying, *'You young people of nowadays, your eyes are too big!'* She always rolled her eyes when she heard that. The fact is, old people didn't understand. If you worked hard, you deserved to play hard. YOLO! You only live once, *abi*? As long as you were smart enough to earn a living and keep making more money, being poor was not your portion, IJN.

Except now, Zuri could see that some savings would have come in handy to take care of the financial black hole laid out in front of her. She worked hard so she could one day enjoy the lifestyle she had always desired—living comfortably in the best part of town, never having to worry about bills, a designer wardrobe that would rival fashion icon Toke Makinwa, shopping trips to Paris and month-long summers in the South of France. To her, that was the ideal life.

It wasn't like she expected to own a home or anything at this point in her life; that, was the responsibility of her future husband. Still, she had no land, no stock portfolio, or anything else that had real value to speak of. There were no assets she could sell to keep her head above water.

What about my bags? Zuri thought. She knew there were some excellent pieces in there, which she had collected over time... Chanel, Alexander McQueen, Céline, and Louis Vuitton bags she didn't even carry anymore. *Chai! How exactly will I sell them?* She wasn't sure there was even a market for used designer bags in Lagos. Everyone was too proud, and if she started asking friends and acquaintances to buy them from her, it would certainly be an indication that something was seriously wrong—then the rumours and gossip would start. There had to be another way.

Her doorbell rang. *Tami!* She was supposed to have lunch with her at Casper & Gambini's. She had seriously been craving one of their famous burgers all week but her new circumstances were cramping her style. She had to re-evaluate her spending. But before she tackled that problem, first she had to figure out how she was going to explain this to Tami.

She went to open the door. Tami stood there, arms folded across her chest. Zuri forced a smile. "Hey! Babe, sorry *oh*, I completely forgot about our lunch plans!"

Tami rolled her eyes. "Forgot, *ke*?"

"Trust me! The *gbese* I'm trying to sort out right now is doing my head in."

She could say this to Tami; they had been best friends for years and spoke freely with each other. Anyone else in Lagos, it was best to keep your mouth shut and pretend everything was great... *before dem carry your matter.*

"Well, I'm coming in because I'm starving," Tami said. Zuri stepped back and let her friend head straight to the kitchen.

They'd met just before they started secondary school in Benin City. They had seen each other through common entrance exams, boy drama, dramatic weight gains and the battle to lose it all, but they were the complete opposite of each other so it was a wonder their friendship had lasted so long.

She was one of those friends you shouldn't attend a party with if your intention was to spend time together, especially if you were the quiet type—she would leave you hanging! It would start with a string of 'hello darlings!', quickly followed by a series of air kisses with eighty percent of the guests at the party, leading to her being dragged from one meaningless conversation to the next, and ending with leaving her partner stranded. It was never intentional, but it was always annoying. Zuri shook her head ruefully.

Tami was an extrovert, the charismatic social butterfly in their group of friends. People were drawn to her; she had flawless caramel-coloured skin, a petite frame, and a smile that could stop most men in their tracks. It wasn't her beauty that drew most people to her, though. She had such a genuine spirit, such a giving aura about her, that people liked her instantly. She was also fiercely loyal, which was probably why their friendship had lasted so long.

Zuri actually felt slightly better about her situation knowing she had someone to confide in and distract her from her money woes.

Plus, Tami always had gist, so it was a welcome distraction.

The sound of Tami slamming the refrigerator door interrupted Zuri's thoughts.

"So you don't even have food in this house?" Tami said with mock disdain in her voice.

"*You no hear say I no get money?*" Zuri laughed.

Tami rolled her eyes. "When I say find a rich boyfriend, you won't hear!"

"Leave me alone, *jo*," Zuri said.

"Girrrl, if you had a man, all this would be story." Tami smiled. "How much is the bill?"

"Not bill—*bills*," Zuri said. "And they add up to just over a million naira."

Tami's eyes widened.

"Seriously, Tami, I don't know how I'm going to get out of this mess. Even if my salary hits my account today, I still won't be able to pay them all."

Tami shook her head. "Honestly, you need to get a man. You need someone to support you. All this independent woman nonsense you are doing is what will get you in trouble. I've always told you, your parents let you stay in *obodo oyinbo* too long. Living abroad for so long is what has got you thinking like an *oyinbo* woman. This is Nigeria, so you better start behaving like an African woman."

Zuri laughed. Tami had a policy never to date married men, but the men she did go out with definitely had to be rich and in a position to help her—gifting her with upper class tickets to whatever destination tickled her fancy, rent for her studio, and closets full of labels from time to time. She was a successful fashion designer and worked from a tiny studio in Lekki, but Zuri was pretty sure Tami's lifestyle was supplemented by her very wealthy father and the string of rich boyfriends she had dated since university.

"Let me give you gist," Tami said. "Do you remember Amanda from high school? She was a few years ahead of us. Tall, light-skinned?"

"Vaguely."

"You are so annoying! You never remember anything. She was friends with Adesuwa and that lot!"

Zuri nodded. "Yeah. Okay, yeah, I remember her. I didn't know her well, but what did she do?"

"She has hit!" Tami clapped her hands together gleefully. "She is dating Seni Foster, the CEO of Foster Inc. and a big boy in the oil sector. He bought her a BMW, a flat in Parkview, and, apparently, a flat in St. John's Wood in London. All in the space of eighteen months!"

Zuri stared at her for a second. "But... isn't he married? I could have sworn I saw pictures of him and his wife on BellaNaija, attending that Balogun wedding in Dubai a few weeks ago."

"Married... fire! So?" Tami hissed. "Why are you acting as if it's news! None of these Lagos big boys are faithful to their wives. Don't be so naïve!"

Zuri rolled her eyes. "He is hardly a *boy*, Tami. Isn't he in his fifties?"

"It doesn't matter! He has money, so he is a Lagos big boy! Finish! Anyway, that was not the point of my story. Amanda is now in the big leagues! I hear he is so in love with her, he is even ready to marry her as a second wife. Word on the street is, he is begging her to have a baby with him."

"*Haba*, Tami! A married man? Stop it! He can't want her to have his babies. I'm pretty sure that part is a lie." Zuri couldn't imagine ever settling to be a man's second wife.

"Listen! You are here, complaining about a bill of one million naira. If you had a boyfriend like that, do you think you would be sitting here trying to figure out how to get out of debt? Not that I subscribe to dating married men, but rich men *sha*..." Tami laughed. "Anyway, I have to get going—I need to eat! And it doesn't look like I'm going to find anything here."

"*Pele*, dear! I got carried away with this money *wahala*!" Zuri laughed.

"Okay," Tami accepted with a wink. "Maybe by next week you'll have met a rich boyfriend," she teased as she waved good-bye.

After Tami left, Zuri began to wonder if she was truly naïve or overly conservative. Was it wrong to think that there was something fundamentally wrong about trading sex for money? The problem with those sorts of relationships though was the power dynamics. In relationships where one was always on the receiving end of the cash, money often became a weapon. She did not want to be controlled. Then she realised that maybe the joke was on her. She was sitting in her living room judging someone who had all their bills paid while she had no clue how she was going to pay her own.

She thought of Folabi, a mistake she had made in her early twenties. A mutual friend introduced them and she was mesmerised by his swag and attitude to life. He wasn't handsome in a conventional way, but he carried himself with a confidence that drew people in. Back then, all the girls wanted to date him and all the guys wanted to be friends with him. Some of it probably had to do with the fact that he was the son of a billionaire and he certainly thought the world revolved around him. Folabi Tajudeen thought he was entitled to behave badly because he had a lot of money to throw around.

They dated for almost a year and she definitely got free trips to New York and London out of it, as well as some really expensive bags, but his arrogance and lack of direction put her off. He was spoiled, with no future ambition of his own. As far as Folabi was concerned, his parents' money meant he didn't actually have to work for a living. Eventually, Zuri realised, despite all the luxuries his money could afford her, she couldn't respect a man who had no ambition of his own and expected to sponge off his parents for his entire life.

His behaviour was appalling and in the end it was an incident that occurred outside Club 57 that became the straw that broke the camel's back. Zuri found it extremely irritating that he had to shout 'do you know who my father is' to make a point to the bouncer, who had told them they had to wait outside because the club was at capacity. She realised that she couldn't respect a man like that, no matter how much money he had access to. She wanted to be with a man that had ambition—at the very least, ambition that exceeded her own—and was willing to work hard to make his dreams come true.

After Folabi, she dated Paul, who was extremely ambitious but that didn't work out either. Zuri sighed as she remembered how excited she had been when they first met at a Euro Money workshop in Paris. Paul got her attention on the first day of the workshop; she was caught off guard by his extreme good looks and easy charm. They were the only Nigerians on the program, so they naturally gravitated toward each other. She was intrigued by how engaging their conversations were. He was smart, funny and devastatingly handsome and it was 'love *wan tin tin*' until their relationship began to unravel a few months later.

Paul was a hustler and she loved that about him. He was a true example of the Nigerian dream. He lost his dad at a very young age and things were very tough for him and his six siblings growing up in Ebonyi, but he clawed his way out of poverty by studying hard and leveraging on every opportunity that came his way. He studied engineering at University of Awka in Anambra state, and then landed a scholarship to pursue a master's degree at the University of Texas. He had risen to be vice president at CIS, a reputable private equity firm in Lagos and was doing quite well for himself but he seemed to have a chip on his shoulder. It wasn't obvious at first because he seemed so comfortable in who he was. However, months later it became obvious that in his bid to adopt a certain 'Lagos big boy' persona, he lied about everything—big things, small things, it didn't seem to matter. It didn't take Zuri long to realise that you couldn't build a solid relationship with someone you couldn't trust at all.

They could be having drinks with a group of friends and she would overhear him telling someone he was going to South Africa at the weekend because he had a big meeting with some tech guys, when she knew for a fact he was going to Ebonyi to visit his family. At first she found it hilarious but as the incidents increased, she got irritated by the fact that he wasn't comfortable in who he was, he was ashamed of his background and found the need to pretend and lie for no apparent reason. Eventually, they broke up when she realised that she had developed the habit of second guessing his every sentence. It got to a point that if Paul told her the sky was blue she would have to check, in case it was actually red. It was difficult to build a relationship with someone you couldn't trust.

Zuri shook her head, trying to clear her thoughts. She didn't want to be thinking about old boyfriends right now. But it was funny, wasn't it? How a conversation about money almost always turned into a conversation about men? *All join* in the *wahala*!

It seemed like something that was culturally engrained in African women, the idea that money was not fundamentally a woman's issue—it was a man's role to worry about finances. If a woman "tabled" the matter of money troubles with her friends, the solution was almost always find a man to look after you. It occurred to her that if a man had confided in his friends or family the similar situation she was in, their advice wasn't likely to be "go and find a sugar mummy".

Zuri was certain that a man was not the answer to her problem. She wasn't ready to date married men like Seni for money or rely on self-obsessed "boy-men" like Folabi, or men with a chip on their shoulder like Paul. None of those scenarios fit the fairy tale ending she had always dreamed of. She would figure a way out of this situation herself. The man she was meant to be with would show up when God said it was time. She was smart, educated and her future was bright.

"I *gat* this," she said, trying to psych herself up.

She just needed to figure a way out of being broke. Simple math: Either make more money or cut back on spending. She needed to raise money to get out of this financial mess—the question was, how?

SMART MONEY LESSON: WHAT "BROKE" REALLY MEANS!

In Sub-Saharan Africa, less than one percent are born into wealth and under ten percent are born into the middle class. In general, we are not taught in any formal framework how to keep money or grow it—basic personal finance skills are difficult to learn. As a result, even when a young adult starts earning more than they need to survive, they end up living from paycheque to paycheque because they think about their incomes largely in terms of spending and haven't learned how to save or build assets in proportion to what they earn.

Broke means, if you lost your primary source of income today, you wouldn't be able to maintain the lifestyle you have become accustomed to because you have no assets to rely on. Like Zuri, many people have built expensive lives they can't sustain because they continuously spend everything they earn and as such, have a revolving door for their money.

We must dismiss this idea that we will always make more money. We have a finite amount of productive years to work; many people will never be as agile both mentally and physically as they are now. What happens in thirty years when you can no longer work as hard and have no cushion to fall back on? Poverty and dependence on others is inevitable. In order to build wealth, this mentality has to change. Developing a wealthy mind-set requires the understanding of the concept that the way you spend, invest, and manage ten naira is the way you'll spend, invest, and manage ten million.

What it Really Means to Be Wealthy

As a society, we tend to measure financial success based on spending patterns, but our metrics are faulty. For example, Zuri lives in one of the best parts of Lagos, has a decent job and lives a lifestyle that many dream of. Zuri is one of the hundreds of thousands moving up the income-earning scale, able to afford material things that were once out of their parents' reach. To a bystander, she has an enviable life and there's an automatic assumption that she is wealthy. However, building wealth is more about how much you *keep*.

Broke people and rich people approach the same amount of money differently and here's why: broke people think it is about how much you earn but rich people know it's about how much of your income you are able to keep and convert into assets that can provide you with an income in the future. The fundamental difference is that wealthy people understand the relationship between how we earn and how we spend and they know where the balance is.

Active income is the income you get from services rendered, it is usually your income from your job or business. For example, if you work at a bank and you make three hundred thousand a month as your salary, that's your active income. Or, if you run a catering business and you make three hundred thousand in profits every month that's your active income.

Passive income in simple terms is money that you make while you are sleeping. It is the income you get regularly from investments you've already made. Good examples are dividends from a stock portfolio, or rental income from a property you own.

What Is Financial Freedom?

When passive income exceeds your expenses.

Ideally, the goal is to get to a point where the assets you've accumulated can pay you enough of an income to pay for your lifestyle. For example, rental income from a property you own can buy you a car or a holiday to the South of France. Or, the dividend cheques from your stock portfolio can buy you a Chanel bag.

EXERCISE: NET WORTH

Calculate your net worth. Your net worth is your assets minus your liabilities and it gives you a snapshot of where you stand financially.

1. Make a list of everything you own of value (stocks, property, land, fixed deposits, cash, gold).

2. Make a list of everything you owe (mortgage, car loan, general gbese).

3. Subtract your total assets from your total liabilities.

4. Don't be ashamed or afraid of the number. Calculating your net worth now will let you know your starting point.

5. The figure is not as important as the trends in net worth. As long as you make a commitment to keep growing it, you'll be fine.

CHAPTER 2:
MONEY FEARS

It was 3:00 a.m. in the morning and Zuri was staring at the ceiling as the latest episode of 'Scandal' flickered on her television screen. She couldn't sleep; her mind kept bouncing from one random thought to another. This was the third week in a row that she'd had to reach for her sleeping pills at this ungodly hour after several futile attempts at sleep. The last couple of weeks she had been worried sick about her money situation. Even though she thought about nothing else these days, a solution wasn't forthcoming and the problems certainly weren't going away.

Mr Okeke, her landlord, had been calling for weeks. He had left message upon message with the security guards saying they had to meet soon. He even rang her bell twice that week but she pretended not to be home. Zuri cringed. It was mortifying. Even her mechanic Ola had been calling her nonstop and had resorted to sending her so many WhatsApp messages, she'd had to block him. But she couldn't hide forever. *That WhatsApp is too intrusive* sef, she thought.

Zuri wasn't ready to deal with any of them yet until she found a solution. She had even started having nightmares about meeting Mr Right and discovering she had infertility issues. She didn't need a shrink to tell her what the dreams meant. They were obviously a symptom of her refusal to confront her fibroids. She had cancelled four appointments with her doctor because, let's face it, she wouldn't be able to pay.

She drifted into a fitful sleep then jolted awake when her alarm went off at 6:00. As she struggled to get dressed for work, she stared at her face in the mirror. Her skin had never looked worse because she hadn't had her regular facial with Dr Bruce at Oasis Med Spa in months. She turned to her favourite pick-me-up; a glycolic skin care treatment that was only available from YoutopiaBeauty.com. Not that she would be able to afford any of that anytime soon.

At 7:40, her Uber driver called to say he was at the gate. As Ola still had her car in his shop, she now had to take taxis to work—yet another expense she could ill afford. She stared out the window as the Toyota Camry drove past the Lekki-Ikoyi tollgate, and she soon tuned out the driver's chatter about his family and the stress of driving in Lagos.

She mentally ran through a list of potential loan sources. *What about Folabi?* Her ex had been reaching out a lot lately to hang out, but that sort of "hanging out" probably meant between the sheets. To make matters worse, if she asked him for the money, he would most certainly expect sex as collateral for the loan. And really, was she that desperate yet?

Then again, Folabi had quite the big mouth. Within a week the whole of Lagos would know he had given her money, and what she had given him in return. His ex, Sheila, had learned the hard way when he boasted about "changing her parade" and buying her first ticket abroad. *Why am I even considering it? Turning aṣewo for a loan?* Ye*!*

When she got to work, Thelma the receptionist beamed at her as she breezed past. "Good morning, Zuri. I love your dress."

"Thank you, love," Zuri replied with a faint smile.

Thelma was a very sweet girl but all *na wash*. She was a newbie, so she wanted to stay in everyone's good graces. Zuri knew her face looked like crap because she had been too exhausted to bother with full makeup this morning but her dress *was* lovely—It was a red Carina dress from one of her favourite Nigerian designers, Lady Biba. It hid her insecurities—like the slight bulge in her lower stomach—and accentuated her best assets. Frankly she felt like a boss lady every time she wore a Lady Biba dress. The dress gave her the confidence boost she needed to participate in this project meeting with her boss that she was now twenty minutes late to. He was going to have a fit! Lateness was something he abhorred and she didn't even have the energy to defend herself.

"We were wondering when you would join us," Mr Tunde said when she arrived. "This meeting started at 8:00 a.m. and it is now 8:25!"

"I'm sorry sir, there was traffic," she said as she hurriedly plugged in her flash drive to begin her presentation.

"Madam, this is Lagos; there is always traffic. Please, let's start with your presentation on the Georgia Heights development."

As Zuri ran through her presentation, it dawned on her that the empty-looking presentation was unimpressive. Still, she stumbled through the best she could, but she knew she was in for it when Mr Tunde told her that he wanted to speak to her.

* * *

Did I make a mistake hiring this returnee? Was all that was running through Mr Tunde's head as he watched her fumble through her half-baked presentation. Zuri Guobadia had worked for the firm for three years and she was clearly a smart girl, but she'd never quite reached the superstar status he'd expected of her. What worried him the most was her complacency.

That is the problem with these returnees; they think they are too smart. As far as he was concerned, they all thought that their fancy degrees were all they needed. They expected fat salaries, no real experience just 'fone' and their degrees. Frankly he was sick of it. He had fired a few of them last year; those ones had had no work ethic. Zuri was one of the last; to be honest she didn't act as entitled as the others but he expected more from her. When she first joined the firm she was eager to please and she closed more sales than he expected from a new comer.

She'd been impressive from the first, sharp with personal allure that had made her a hit with the clients. She'd also been a hit with some of the senior partners too, but she'd made it quite clear that her rise to the top would be completely by merit, not favouritism.

Mr Tunde chuckled as he recalled the first hundred-million-naira sale Zuri had closed right in front of him. It had been Mr Obako, one of those clients who had millions of dollars in the bank, showed avid interest whenever Richmond Developments completed a new development, requested countless meetings but never managed to actually buy anything.

The company only entertained his requests because there was always a possibility of a sale, since he actually had money and he was good friends with several influential members of the board. He had put Zuri on this particular account because none of the other senior partners would touch it and she seemed personable enough to manage Obako's quirks. He had joined the meeting with the intention of observing her sales pitch and to give her some follow up tips. Instead he'd been shocked by the finesse of her delivery and the way she skilfully dealt with Obako's inane questions. That day, Mr Tunde knew she had the makings of a star.

For the past eighteen months however, he'd felt as though Zuri's star was more than just a bit tarnished. Her performance was average and it looked like she had plateaued and was content to keep coasting. She wasn't present and definitely wasn't engaged. The ambition and hunger to learn that had seemed to possess her when she first started at the firm had obviously left her.

Mr Tunde felt invested in her development, because in some ways he thought of himself as Zuri's unofficial mentor, but every attempt to get her to get back in the game had been met with excuses. For the past two years he had nominated her as one of the delegates to attend a conference the company sponsored. Women in Management, Business and Public service or more simply, WIMBIZ, was the largest and most substantial women's organisation in Nigeria that played a significant role in empowering working Nigerian women. He thought it would be great for her development but each year, she came up with weak excuses why she couldn't attend. This year he wouldn't give her the option.

* * *

Zuri tapped nervously as she waited. She knew she'd been late, but it hadn't been *that* late! And yes, her presentation had been a bit shoddy, but it wasn't like she was generally incompetent. *He should give me a break* jo! Zuri thought, exasperated. The last thing she needed today was a lecture from the self-righteous Mr Tunde. He was a great boss for the most part, but he could be a real pain in the ass some times.

"I was very disappointed in your presentation today—you mixed up a lot of the details," said Mr Tunde. "In fact, if I'm honest, you haven't done any good work in months." He frowned. "I don't know what's going on with you, but you need to get your act together!"

Zuri had the grace to look shamefaced. "I'm sorry sir, I'll admit I was ill prepared but it won't happen again."

Mr Tunde shook his head. "That's what you said the last few times you've come to my meetings with substandard work. You are on the end of a very short rope and I'm tempted to sack you. In these harsh economic times, we have no room for slackers and I don't carry passengers on my team.

"Everyone has to perform! I had high hopes for you, Zuri, but recently, you just seem to be completely okay with mediocrity."

He shook his head again. "That's the problem with you returnees—you expect fat salaries for mediocre work. You want to furnish these lavish lifestyles but not put in the effort that's required. I put you on this account because Obako is a difficult client and I knew that if you applied yourself, you'd be able to handle it but you haven't applied yourself—you're just coasting along. You're doing what you need to do to survive and nothing more."

He looked at her closely. "Zuri you have become complacent and it's rather worrying, but then again maybe real estate isn't what you want to do anymore."

Zuri's heart skipped a beat. No. She couldn't be fired right now. "It is sir, it is."

She looked at him, doing her best not to say too much for fear of bursting into tears. Her body was hot from embarrassment and she was choking up with unshed tears. Mr Tunde might be a nag and a bit grumpy, but was one of the greatest proponents of her success since she joined the firm, showing her the ropes and honing her skills. She hated to admit it but his opinion mattered to her. His respect mattered to her.

"I think you need something to... how do the kids say it these days? *Ginger* you! You need a fresh perspective so I have nominated you as one of the delegates for this year's WIMBIZ conference," Mr Tunde said. "The theme is leadership—stepping up and standing out."

Zuri raised her eyebrows. This was an unpleasant surprise; she couldn't bear the thought of going to one of "those" women conferences. This was not the first time that he had tried to get her to go to WIMBIZ, but she wasn't a fan of organisations like it because they seemed very political and cliquey, and she felt like the women who were interested in going to such events had to be ready to suck up to powerful women. Although she had never attended WIMBIZ before, she had attended a few similar conferences in the early days of her move back to Nigeria and they were boring, to say the least.

As she opened her mouth to protest, she saw the disapproving look on Mr Tunde's face and decided against it. Now was not the time to test him.

"Attend the conference this year and write a report about everything you learned and give us feedback about business trends and the workshops you participate in. Is that clear?"

"Yes, sir."

"Good. Then you may go." He scowled as he waved her out of his office.

***

As she stood at her front door that evening and riffled through her Céline tote to find her keys, she heard footsteps approaching. At first she thought it was one of her neighbours but then she heard Mr Okeke's thick Igbo accent apparently talking to someone on his phone. "*Nne*, let me call you back, I *don* see who I *dey* find!"

She was caught! She wouldn't be able to find the house keys fast enough to get into the house and pretend she hadn't noticed him. Besides, he had this look in his eyes like he meant business and had no problem disgracing her in front of all the neighbours.

"Good evening, Mr Okeke." Zuri tried to sound confident despite the deep embarrassment she felt.

"Good evening, *abi?* Madam. What is good about the evening when you've been running away from paying *ya* service charge? Tell me what is good about the evening?" His voice grew louder and by the time he'd finished speaking he was bellowing.

Zuri felt her face flush but she struggled to stay calm and push her guilt out of the way. "Uhm, Mr Okeke, how am I running away?"

"Madam, I have come here over ten times this month looking for you," Mr Okeke sneered. "You have clearly been dodging me, but let me tell you something: if you don't pay me this week, I will cut off your power and water supply. Then how good will your evenings be? You are trying the wrong person! You think this place is free?! Do you know how much it costs me to maintain this building? I can't afford for small girls like you to be owing me, and, to make matters worse, you've been avoiding my phone calls!"

"Mr Okeke, please lower your voice." Zuri saw her nosey neighbour, Mrs B, looking out of her kitchen window and began to panic. If this situation escalated any further, she would be the sole topic of conversation in the compound for the next couple of weeks. Who knew where the gist would spread to. She felt like sinking into the ground.

"I should lower my voice, *abi*? Look at this stupid girl *oh*, instead of you to tell me how you are going to pay me my money you are saying I should lower my voice."

"Please calm down *oga*, I will pay you," Zuri pleaded.

"I should calm down? You are very stupid. I don't blame you—I blame the *aristo* that paid your rent."

Zuri recoiled in shock. "Which *aristo*? I have a job! How dare you! I don't sleep with men for money, I'm just having some financial challenges but I will pay you. You don't have to insult me!"

"All you small girls that will be sleeping with big men for money, then come to Lekki Phase I to pay rent you cannot sustain." Mr Okeke shook his head in disgust. "I'm sure you have quarrelled with the baba you were sleeping with that's why you can't come up with the money. Look your rent will be due in less than three months. If you can't pay service charge, how can I expect my rent money?"

She stared at him in utter disbelief as he continued his rant. He had the gall to say that to her face! "Mr Okeke, it is enough!" she shouted. For the first time that evening, he was silent.

"I did not kill anybody. I owe you, and I am telling you, I will pay! When my salary comes at the end of the month, I will pay half of what I owe and find another means of paying the rest in the next couple of weeks. I am very sorry to have put you in this position but please don't ever speak to me in this manner again. That I owe you is not license for you to disrespect me!"

Mr Okeke appeared too dumbfounded to say anything. Zuri took a deep breath as her hand closed on her keys at the bottom of her bag.

"Have a good evening," she said as she unlocked her door, entered her flat and closed the door in his face.

What a mess. What a huge mess.

Later that night, as she sank into her five hundred-thread count Egyptian cotton sheets to try and fall asleep, she knew she had just taken the first steps toward solving her money problems. She had confronted the biggest and most threatening debt, taken control of the situation, come up with a plan—and the sky had not fallen! Although she hadn't yet paid the debt, she fell asleep with a strong conviction in her mind that she would.

* * *

"Hello, Mummy! How are you?" Zuri said into the phone as she attempted to sound cheerful. She didn't want her mother to worry about her.

"I'm wonderful. We Thank God! How is Lagos? How is work? I hope you are going to church, *oh*?"

"Yes, Mummy, I am. Work is fine and Lagos is fine. How are things in Benin?"

As she listened to her mother rant about PHCN not providing electricity for over a week, her lower back pain and weekly doctor's visits, Zuri felt horrible about what she was about to ask her mum.

It had been a week since she realised her bills had piled up and the pressure from her landlord, as well as not having a functioning car to go to work, was starting to get to her. She had attempted to "tax" her older brothers Osahon and Nehikhare, who both lived abroad with their families, but they had both been *posting* her all week.

Osahon lived in Russia, had a Russian wife (who seemed lovely) and two beautiful girls. Zuri had never met them in person because they had never visited Nigeria, so her relationship with them was mostly via Skype and email. When she'd called Osahon to ask for money, he'd told her things were tight and he had just sent money to Benin for Mummy, so he didn't have any spare cash but he would see what he could do. That was a week ago.

Nehikhare lived in Texas. When she spoke to him last week, he'd complained bitterly about his crippling student loans from pursuing both a first degree and a masters, and how he'd had to rely on his credit card just to be able to make ends meet this month. So, no money from that end either.

I hate what I'm about to do. Her mother was a widow, their father having died many years ago. Mama Osahon (as Zuri's mother was often called) survived on her husband's meagre civil service pension and proceeds selling fabric in New Benin market. Her income was supplemented by money her sons sent every couple of months. The woman wasn't hungry but she certainly wasn't in a position to be funding a grown daughter's bad decisions.

"Are you listening?" Zuri's mother asked. "I said, Aunty Uwa is coming to Lagos next week on her way to New York, should I send you fruits? Or yam?"

"No Mummy, I'm good. Thank you!" She was brought back to the present. She took a deep breath. "Mummy, please can you loan me some money?"

"How much?" her mum asked.

"About five hundred thousand naira. I'm really broke," Zuri replied. "Mummy, you know I wouldn't ask if it wasn't important."

She couldn't bring herself to ask for the full amount because for starters, she knew her mother didn't have that kind of disposable income and she also didn't want her to get too worried about her.

"*Ha.* Broke *ke*? How can you be broke? Aren't you working? *Abi* did you lose your job? What do you need five hundred thousand for anyway?"

Zuri's explanation was met with a series of sighs on the other end of the line.

"My dear, I'm not in any position to help you right now. As I told you earlier, we've been spending so much money on diesel in this house because of the electricity situation and my hospital bill is still pending, but let me see if I can borrow from Aunty Uwa."

"No mummy, don't ask her. I will figure it out."

"How?! You just said you have no money."

"It doesn't matter," Zuri said, trying to reassure her. "I'm expecting some money in a few weeks I just wanted something to tide me over in the meantime." A lie, of course. She had no idea how she was going to find the money.

It took Zuri another hour to get her mother off the phone and reassure her that things weren't that bad. But they were and the question that kept replaying in her mind was, *how did things end up like this?*

Zuri was loath to admit to herself, but she couldn't escape the truth: she had been careless about her money. She always assumed that as long as she had a great job she would never be hungry. At the back of her mind, her back up plan was the Bank of the Family Bailout. Unfortunately, they were closed for business
She'd even thought about going to her friends, cap in hand, but she had enough pride not to go down that road. Even Tami who was

closest to her, had heard her story but didn't offer to help and Zuri recognised that it was probably because Tami didn't have that kind of disposable income to lend.

As Zuri stared at her bank balance for the hundredth time, she finally understood being completely and utterly broke. Her version of broke didn't come from not having a job or being a low-income earner, it came from being bad with money. She had been working for eight years and had no assets to show for her hard work—a measly amount of cash in the bank, no land, no stocks. Nothing of value to fall back on when thing got bad, and things were disastrous.

SMART MONEY LESSON

There's a lot of fear surrounding the way African women feel about money and the subsequent consequences of our relationship with money. When it comes to money in relation to our families, our businesses, our friendships, and society, many African women worry about not having enough to survive, not having enough to measure up to the lifestyle of our friends and family, the fear of failing in business, the fear of not being able to afford the lifestyle one has become accustomed to, then losing it all and becoming dependent on others.

Ultimately how we behave with money is deeply rooted in how we think about money and fear can be a very crippling thing; it can stifle you and stop you from taking action to achieve your goals but we must realise that fear is just an emotion. It is worrying about something that has the possibility to occur in the future. Unfortunately, this fear can be paralysing. So sometimes instead of confronting and facing those money fears, we hide from them and avoid them. However, confronting our fears is always the right step toward conquering them.

What you deny or ignore, you delay; what you accept and face, you conquer. At the end of the day we are all afraid of something but the difference between successful people and average people is that they acknowledge their fears but don't let fear overcome them or stop them from achieving their goals.

EXERCISE: CONQUER MONEY FEARS

1. *Make a list of all your money fears.*
2. *Think about why you have this money fear in the first place. It might be rooted in money habits that you already know are bad for your finances. For example, having expenses that are so high they consistently exceed your income each month, so you know it's not sustainable and there's a voice in the back of your head that tells you you're living beyond your means, hence the fear of not being able to maintain your lifestyle.*
3. *Make a plan to counter each fear. The reason we usually allow fear to take over is because we don't have a plan and are uncertain of what will happen in the future. There is nothing that gives you confidence like having a detailed plan to conquer that uncertainty.*

CHAPTER 3:
WHERE IS YOUR MONEY GOING?

It was a Saturday morning, the day Zuri had set aside to begin the process of tackling her financial situation. A track from MI's new album was blasting from her iPod speakers.

'Ilekun a și,

Ișe owo mi fi alubarika si,
Everything we dey face right now go turn story,
We will all be rich,
We will all be rich.

From cooking with kerosene, to the back of limousine,
Going where we never been to seeing things we never seen.
From buying food inside newspaper to the front page of magazines,

...when they see you tomorrow they won't recognise that they've seen you before,

...I'm wishing you money; I'm wishing you wealth.

She danced around her apartment and sang along to the words. *My ginger is on ten!*

It was odd, but the words from the song gave her hope. Hope that even though she didn't have a clear plan to pay off her debts and find financial stability, she would figure it out eventually because she was motivated.

She had decided to deal with this financial situation the same way she would tackle a task at work—logically! As she sorted through the paper bag that acted as a filing cabinet for all her bank statements and service charge bills, she puzzled over where exactly all her money had gone. She earned about six hundred thousand naira a month, which frankly was a lot of money and way above the average Nigerian salary. So, where was it all going? What was she spending it on?

As she rifled through the bag she noticed that most of her bank statements were unopened. It dawned on Zuri: she'd been supremely careless with her money for an incredibly long time. There had been months at a stretch she hadn't even checked her bank account. The statements she *had* looked at, she'd only paid cursory attention to.

She sorted through the statements, arranged them according to dates and used her highlight pens to categorise her spending. Blue for meals, pink for accessories, green for her car, and so on and so forth. As she pored over her financial life, she came to an even more depressing realisation: she had always been afraid of her bank statements and she hadn't wanted to admit to herself how precarious her life really was. Subconsciously, she'd always known she was spending mindlessly but never wanted to confront her spending habits because it made her uncomfortable.

She told herself that she worked hard and earned good money so she deserved to splurge once in a while, but what was evident from this exercise was that she indulged all the time. Damn! She couldn't believe how much she spent alone on dinner and cocktails with the girls at RSVP and Spice every month!

An exhausted Zuri sat back and stared at the now neat stacks of paper on her dining table. She'd spent hours analysing the statements, trying to make sense of the numbers. It was painful but eye-opening. In fact, she had a new philosophy: if you want to truly know a person, look at their bank statements. Apparently, the picture her bank statements painted was that she was an obese alcoholic with an unhealthy bag addiction, who owned enough *aṣo-ebi* to open her own mall. *Who is Ria and why did I pay so much for her aṣo-ebi for goodness' sake?*

But that wasn't who she was, was it? Why then, did the money she had spent not reflect her values?

She had decided the best way to make sense of everything was to put all the data she had collected under her six biggest spending categories: rent, utilities, food, transportation, wardrobe, and other, and began to make sense of them in relation to her annual income of about seven point two million.

The two point five million she paid annually for her two-bedroom apartment was easily her biggest expenditure. She had read an article once that described Lagos as one of the most expensive cities in the world and she couldn't agree more. The unspoken success and wealth connotations of living on "The Island" had made Phase I one of the more desirable parts of town. Even though she loved living there she couldn't help but think she was living in an up-market ghetto. The bad roads, inefficient power supply, and the sometimes filthy water was not exactly high-class living. Luckily, she was only paying a year's rent upfront; most Nigerians had to pay two.

The utilities were fairly easy to track because she'd been receiving monthly service charge notices from Mr Okeke's facilities manager that detailed the cost of diesel, PHCN, water, security, refuse collection and other maintenance services—these all added up to her quarterly service charge bill. If she added the cost of cable from DStv, her internet subscription, and the amount of money she spent on buying credit for her mobile phone, she was spending roughly five hundred thousand a quarter, which came to about two million a year.

When it came to transportation, it cost about eight thousand a week (or about thirty-two thousand a month to fill the tank of her car), which usually lasted about a week. That translated to four hundred and sixteen thousand a year. If she included the occasional Uber ride—which were lifesavers when there was fuel scarcity or her car was at the mechanic's—she would be spending approximately seven hundred and eighty-four thousand on transportation this year, excluding car repairs.

In her head, she took apart the true expense of her guilty pleasure—her wardrobe.

Shoes. *at an average of one hundred and eighty thousand a pop I've bought at least ten pairs of designer shoes in the last twelve months, which adds up to just over one million. On shoes!*

Aṣo-ebi. Attending weddings for people I don't even know cost me about sixty thousand a month, seven hundred and twenty thousand a year. Haba. *And that's without designer. With "tailor", another four hundred and eighty thousand for the year. For outfits I would never re-rock.*

The more Zuri looked at it, the more ludicrous it seemed to her, the pomp and circumstance of being a wedding guest. If you attended a wedding, you had to wear the *aṣo-ebi* as a symbol of your support of the bride and groom. In some cases, you may not even be allowed to enter the venue for the wedding reception if you were not wearing said *aṣo-ebi*!

As she caught a glimpse of one of her Virgos Lounge dresses peeking out of her closet, she did a quick calculation on everything in the last batch of wardrobe expenses: Nigerian designers.

She had spent a pretty penny shopping at Zazaii, the new department store on Balarabe Musa. She had spent one point eight million on outfits in less than twelve months! It wasn't that the pieces she bought were particularly expensive; it was the frequency of her purchases. You could say many things about the city of Lagos, but it was never boring. There were events every weekend. If it wasn't a wedding, there was some kind of fashion event or new restaurant opening and every event required a new outfit to kill on the red carpet and make it on to the blogs like on BellaNaija or Linda Ikeji. The comment sections of *Naija* blogs were always brutal.

Zuri stared at the Excel sheet on her MacBook Pro that now had detailed information on how she had spent her income in the past twelve months. She was an odd mix of fear, annoyance, depression, and excitement. She had no savings, no assets, and that worried her. She would have to get serious about her finances and be disciplined if she wanted to get herself out of this situation and not repeat her mistakes. It frightened her if she was being completely honest, but it made one thing clear; she was going to have to go on a money diet and first up was to clear her debt to Mr Okeke.

Even though a plan to tackle the imminent threat of her debt had begun to form in her head, Zuri still felt at sea. She knew she would have to make some changes to her spending if she was going to be on track in the long run. She had to forgive herself for her money mistakes; they were in her past and what mattered was that she was doing something about it now.

As she considered how brutal her spending diet was going to be in the next few months, her thoughts were interrupted by a loud banging on the door. PHCN had decided they weren't going to provide electricity today and so the doorbell wasn't working. She wondered who it was. She wasn't expecting any guests but the banging was a little too familiar.

"*Abeg hold oh, abi na you get* house?" Zuri shouted.

As she looked through the peephole she realised it was her security guard.

"Suleiman what is it now? why are you banging my door like that?"

"Sorry ma, I been *tink* say you no fit hear as light no *dey*," he said in a placating tone.

"Person come drop something for you," he said as he handed her a rather large but fancy gold gift box.

"Thank you."

This looks suspiciously like aṣo-ebi*. The packaging for these things* *are becoming fancier with each passing wedding.* For the life of her, Zuri couldn't think of whose wedding it could be. She didn't remember paying for any recently.

As she read the card that came with the box, she felt even more confused. *Hashtag: #AbeTa,* ke? "You are invited to Abena and Tayo's wedding," the card read.

As the realisation hit, she started dialling a number on her phone.

"Hi darling, what's popping?"

"Tami! Why is Abena sending me *aṣo-ebi*? Are we friends? I mean I've only met the girl a handful of times. Wait. How did she even get my address?"

"Calm down, what's the big deal! She said she wanted to invite you to the wedding and asked me for your address," Tami laughed. "I thought it was nice of her."

"Nice?! I don't have money to be paying for *aṣo-ebi* right now. *Abi* is it free? if it's free that's fine. Besides when did people start sending *aṣo-ebi* before payment?"

"Zuri, you are over reacting. It's just thirty thousand."

"Uhm, I've told you what my financial situation is like right now, so there's no "just" with one kobo of my money right now. I spent the last couple of hours going through my bank statements and it turns out 'just thirty thousand' translates to a lot of money over a period of time. I've decided I'm only buying *aṣo-ebi* for close friends' weddings. Otherwise it's such a waste."

Tami was roaring with laughter. "I'd like to see how you would pull that off, with weddings every other weekend in this Lagos. I'm not even sure what you are complaining about. I'm one of her bridesmaids and if you see the list of demands, you'll cry. There's the cost of the bridesmaids' dresses, she'd like us to wear matching Sophia Webster shoes, there's the money we have to contribute to her hen night and bridal shower. *Abeg,* the list is long! Before it's over I will have spent at least three hundred thousand and you are complaining about thirty thousand."

"That is just ridiculous. When you are not the one getting married?"

"Darling, it's what you do for friends. Remember that one day you will get engaged and expect other people to pay for your own."

"Trust me, with what I'm going through now, I doubt I'll be subjecting other people to any unrealistic demands when it's my turn."

As she got off the phone, Zuri began to make a list of all the things she had to quit spending on if she had any real chance of paying Mr Okeke.

Goodbye ProFlex gym membership, she thought. Even though she loved the way Jide's Longevity classes made her feel, she knew she had to make some sacrifices in the medium term. She could re-join later, but for now, running on the Lekki-Ikoyi Bridge would have to do. At least that one was free.

'Other' was a huge category for her. It mostly included money she had withdrawn from the ATM and she couldn't account for properly because she had a hazy recollection of how the cash was spent. Tips, petrol, a quick stop at the grocery store when their point of sales machines weren't working. Still, Zuri decided she would limit herself to twenty thousand cash a week and make it a point to make a note on her iPhone each time she spent cash. She would also put herself on a budget for her phone; she was definitely spending a lot on credit and data, having meaningless telephone and FaceTime conversations with her friends.

It went without saying that she was on a clothes purchasing ban for at least six months. From now on, she would either wear the clothes and shoes she had in her wardrobe, or she would sit her behind at home. Eating out also had to be cut down to only special occasions for the next six months or till she figured herself out.

Zuri decided that avoiding her bank statements and not checking the balance of her accounts were no longer options. She would set money dates with herself on Sundays, to see how much she had spent each week and stay on track with the goals she had set for herself with regards to how she would cut her spending.

Cut spending by fifty percent! She spun in her chair and grinned in relief.

* * *

Zuri was excited about her social life for the first time in weeks. She was having the girls over for dinner instead of going to eat at a restaurant, in a bid to balance her new frugal life style with some much needed fun. She had told them to each bring something—a bottle of wine, a dessert, something—to contribute to the dinner party. They were a rowdy bunch so she knew the night would be full of laughter and fun. God knew she needed a night like this so badly.

She had been on a spending diet for about six weeks since her big *aha!* moment. She had intended to cut her spending by fifty percent but had found it unsustainable. She could only manage to set aside about thirty-five percent from last month's salary, so she had two hundred and ten thousand naira sitting in her savings account. It wasn't nearly enough to cover her debt but it was a good start.

She couldn't even front and pretend to be completely happy, because It had meant cutting out a lot from her life. The spending diet actually felt more like a juice cleanse, but, either way, she was starving. She was trying to make it a habit to keep track of everything she spent in a notebook which she reviewed at the end of every week. If she was honest, it was exhausting! Penny pinching was not her thing. It was hard and she wasn't sure this *'frugalista'* life was for her long-term.

The struggle is real.

She missed her weekly trips to Zazaii to splurge on her favourite Nigerian designers. She'd spotted a new Clan dress on Instagram that she knew she would have bought instantly, if she hadn't put herself on a clothes ban. And, she definitely was experiencing severe bouts of FOMO—the fear of missing out—when she saw pictures of her friends at RSVP having cocktails. If she was being completely honest, she felt deprived and it was exhausting! It had been a tough sell getting the girls to come to her house for dinner on a Friday night instead of heading to the hot new bar that had just opened.

Tami, Lara, Adesuwa, and Ladun had relented after I bombarded them with text messages. They were always so much fun.

It was almost 7:00 p.m. and her guests had started arriving.

"I've always loved this flat. it's *so* chic," Tami said as she sauntered in.

"I know, right? I'm always telling people how Zuri got such a great deal on this flat," Lara said. "It has so much space and it's finished really well. I can't believe you only pay two point five million, especially on this particular street. I've always loved the left side of Lekki Phase I; it's still fairly residential compared to the rest of the estate, which is becoming too commercial."

"Tell me about it," said Ladun as she rolled her eyes. "I don't know how you guys can live here. There's just too much going on at once: Domino's, Ebeano, the filling stations, the traffic! That's why I love living in Ikoyi. None of this mess."

Tami and Zuri shared a telling look. Ladun was an area snob; she thought certain areas in Lagos were beneath her because they were too "pedestrian". She was one of those girls that made annoying statements like 'I don't do the mainland' or 'I only cross Third Mainland Bridge when I have to get to the airport.' This was ironic to the people who knew her before she married Bode (who was from an old-money Lagos family and grew up in Ikoyi) and became 'brand new'. Ladun actually grew up in Ijesha, which was, in fact, on the mainland.

"Hmmm, I don't know, *oh*," Adesuwa chimed in. "It's a really nice flat for sure but don't you think living here is a bad idea for Zuri? I mean, she's single and this is the sort of show of wealth that drives guys away."

Zuri stared at her blankly. She was used to this annoying line of conversation from Adesuwa, because she was one of those women who believed a woman must downplay her achievements to seem more attractive. She had shared with the girls on several occasions how she lied to her husband about how much she earned before they got married. Zuri still could not figure out why a woman had to make herself seem that much smaller to accommodate a man's ego.

Adesuwa was an associate at a top law firm in Lagos and she was married to Soji, who did "business", although it was an open secret that they depended on Adeswua's salary to survive. Still, Adesuwa kept up the charade that Soji was the breadwinner, preserving his pride.

"Should I live under the bridge because I'm single?" said Zuri. "My mother doesn't live in Lagos, and frankly, I like my space! The thought of sacrificing my comfort and living with a distant relative until someone decides to marry me is depressing!"

"*I tire, oh,*" Lara chimed in. "I've never understood that logic! Please, I believe you attract what you want in this life. If a guy is intimidated by the fact that she lives in a two-bedroom flat, then he should keep it moving! That's not the type we are looking for, *abeg!*" She hissed.

"*Abi oh!* Zuri please don't listen to Adesuwa, before you come and attract the type that is hungry and looking at you to feed him!" Ladun laughed.

"This reminds me of a client I had a fitting with today in the studio," Tami said. "She's a banker, she's single, and she was lamenting about how she really wanted to buy a Honda SUV but her mum won't let her—not because she can't afford it but because her mum believes it will make her seem too independent and drive potential suitors away. Can you believe that? I couldn't stop laughing. The girl was so upset!

"That's the society we live in," Adesuwa replied. The women all nodded. "Men generally feel threatened if you seem just as successful as them, or, even worse, if you are *more* successful than them. It's just wisdom when you downplay it!"

"That's not true, *oh*, Adesuwa!' Zuri laughed. "I know lots of Nigerian men who are married to women who are equally as successful as them and they seem very happy! These days no man wants a woman that's a liability."

"I think it's all about finding a balance!" Lara said. "I love earning my own money but I need a man that can look after me! Forget all that fifty-fifty nonsense! My money is my money—his money is our money!"

They all burst into laughter and high-fived each other.

"Plus, I have a Chanel addiction that I fully intend my future husband to fund," she added. "And it would be nice for someone to share some of the financial burden I carry sending my siblings to school. Even though I earn good money, the financial responsibility of looking after my family takes its toll sometimes. And the truth is, I always feel like no matter how much I make I'm spending it on others faster than I can spend it on myself."

Lara was an oil and gas "big babe"—status granted by the fact that she was an oil trader with great pay and a job that took her on regular trips all over the world. She had café-au-lait skin, a tiny waist and generous curves—which went a long way to attract the array of rich men, both single and married, who were constantly sending her gifts. She was always very secretive about her love life, so none of the other girls were ever sure if she was actually dating any of these men, or if they were just rumours based on the guys she'd been seen with around town occasionally. Her father had died when she was very young and, as the eldest child, she had always felt responsible for looking after her mother and three siblings. Even though she earned a lot of money for her age, a good proportion went to paying university fees, plus rent and living expenses for her mum. They were all in awe of her sense of responsibility because even though she complained from time to time, they knew she couldn't see herself doing otherwise.

Zuri was enjoying herself, and she was glad to see that her friends didn't seem to be missing being out at a trendy restaurant. But just as she started to crack open the second bottle of wine, she decided it might be a good idea to share some of her money concerns with the girls.

"Guys, do you ever think about where all your money goes?" Zuri said, suddenly.

Lara laughed. "How? What do you mean?"
"I mean, where does it all go? I work hard, I make decent money but it never seems like it's enough because the bills keep coming! As in,

it never stops. I've been struggling financially the last few weeks and I can't help wondering where does all my money go. In fact, since that incident with my landlord, I've been paying a lot of attention to what I spend my money on and it dawned on me the other day that a lot of the money goes to things that are not necessarily at the top of my priority list."

"Girl, I can relate!" Lara said. "Even with my salary, I feel silly complaining that it's never enough because I have so many expenses every month. Between hospital bills for my mum and school fees for my siblings, my financial obligations are a nightmare. I can't even afford to go on holiday or buy a new car but they are my responsibility so what can I do?"

"I've never really thought about it," Ladun said. "I don't work *oh*, but Bode gives me a healthy allowance but I can't really tell you where it goes specifically."

"Shopping!" the rest of the girls laughed in unison.

Ladun smiled then hissed jokingly. "Don't be funny! Do I shop more than the rest of you?"

"Yes! You do!" Tami replied. "Every conversation with you is about how you absolutely have to get that Dior, Chanel or Louis Vuitton bag you saw so and so girl rocking on Instagram."

"*Ehn*, I like designer bags. So shoot me," Ladun said cheekily. "Bode is not complaining."

"Yes, but we are just pointing out that that's where your money goes," Lara said, still very amused by her friends' antics. "Tami you, *nko*? Where does your money go?"

"*Mehn*, I'll have to say weddings," Tami said. "I don't know if my name is on the internet with a sign that says 'professional bridesmaid'. Almost everyone I know that gets engaged wants me to be on their train! *I don tire*! Plus, it's getting expensive.... But weeeell, I can't lie, *sha*, I'm also addicted to Good Hair. Kika and Chioma sell the nicest hair."

They all laughed and nodded in agreement except Adesuwa, who had gone quiet.

"Adesuwa are you alright?" Zuri said. "You haven't said much. Where does your own money go? Tell us, *na*?"

"Soji." Adesuwa said solemnly.

"What do you mean?" Ladun said, slightly confused.

"I mean, the bulk of my money goes to Soji! Soji and his family members!" Adesuwa said right before she burst into tears.

For a startled moment, no one said anything. They all exchanged worried looks and then Tami rushed to her side to console her. "What's wrong, love? Talk to us. Maybe we can help."

"*Mehn*! I'm just frustrated!" Adesuwa sobbed. "Everything is just a bit much right now."

"What do you mean?" Zuri asked.
Adesuwa took several ragged breaths, then everything came out in a rush. "I mean it's not one particular thing! I just feel overwhelmed

sometimes. I work so hard to earn money so my family is alright, but it always seems like it's never enough. It's always one thing after the other—if the generator doesn't break down this week, there'll be something that needs fixing in one of the cars or a hospital bill for Junior. It just feels never-ending sometimes, like I'm working only to work for even more money to spend on things that don't make me any happier, but just stress the hell out of me. Then there's the anxiety that comes with knowing that we have barely any savings and zero assets to speak of. If I lose my job tomorrow, my family is in serious trouble."

"Have you talked to Soji about this?" Ladun asked.

"I can't!" Adesuwa exclaimed.

Lara, Zuri, Tami, and Ladun all exchanged knowing glances.

"What do you mean you can't?" Ladun said. "He is your husband and he's supposed to support you. You should be able to share this sort of frustration with him, or, better still, this should be his frustration not yours."

Adesuwa sighed. "Listen! The last few months have been really tough on Soji. His new business venture hasn't exactly taken off yet. If I share my frustrations with him, he might see it as me complaining and I don't want that. Don't mind me, you guys, I was just having a moment. It's probably all the wine I drank that's making me emotional. It's just frustrating sometimes because I'm constantly thinking '*What exactly am I working for? Where does all the money go?*' We've been trying to take a vacation for the last three years but by the time we spend the money on all these expenses, there's nothing left over to go to *Ilaṣe*, not to talk of London."

Tami tried to ease the tension. "Girl, I'm sure at one point or the other we all wish that someone would tell us everything would be all right, give us a hug, then hand us a million dollars!"

"Preach!" Zuri giggled as she raised one hand in the air. She poured another glass of wine and set it in front of Adesuwa.

Ladun patted Adesuwa on the shoulder and glanced at the other girls, silently seeking support for what she was going to say next.

"Adesuwa, I think you baby Soji too much! I don't mean to be rude but he's getting too complacent! It's one thing if you are working to contribute fifty-fifty to the household but when you are carrying the burden alone that's not fair! You are the woman, not the man, *oh*! This is why I don't work! Before Bode gets any ideas. It's the man's responsibility to provide for the family and once you upset that dynamic they start to resent you for it. I've seen it happen many times."

Zuri and Tami shifted in their seats uncomfortably.

Adesuwa sobbed. "You don't understand. He is under a lot of stress! He took a loan from the bank for the start-up he was trying to run before he had this new idea and it's already a struggle paying that loan back. He started building a house for his mum, so the pressure there is also adding to his stress. He doesn't want to let her down, so I'm chipping in a good chunk of my salary, but it's stressful because before I cough my salary is finished."

Lara broke her silence. "Ladun has a point, *oh*, Adesuwa! What if you stopped working—then what would Soji do? The things that some men do, *sha*, I don't understand. You have a good woman that's willing to hold you down who's supportive and wants to see you succeed, shouldn't that be an incentive to work harder and stop playing at business? Business is not for everyone, *abeg*! If he's tried these many businesses and they didn't work out, then he can just go and get a job. It is irresponsible! He has children for God's sake."

"*Abi!*" said Ladun. "Plus, Adesuwa, why should it be your responsibility to help him build his mother's house? You are taking things too far! This man obviously thinks you are a *mumu*. Shouldn't his wife and child be his number one priority?"

Adesuwa sighed. "Not every married person is into wealth like you *oh*, Ladun. Soji is his mother's only son, so he sees it as his responsibility to look after her and I actually admire that about him. Do I resent the fact that the financial burden of his responsibility rests on me? Yes, but he is my husband and I love him. It's my duty to support him."

"Let me just tell you, Adesuwa, you are being foolish! Love *ko*, love *ni!*" Ladun scoffed. "You are his wife—not his mother or father. You have your roles mixed up. If he starts giving the money you earn to all these *small small* girls in Lagos, then you will know. Just don't come here and complain, *sha*."

Zuri could tell that her friends were growing uncomfortable with where the conversation was headed. What had happened to her fun, carefree dinner party? Why did the talk always seem to circle back to marriage and money? She glanced at Adesuwa. They had all heard rumours of Soji's infidelity but never discussed it with her, because it was just what a large number of men did in Lagos. In fact, it was almost as though Nigerian women didn't expect fidelity but they also didn't expect it to be thrown in their faces.

Soji's overt infidelity irked because he was also a lousy provider for Adesuwa and Soji Jr. It was as though he spent his time looking for new ways to humiliate her and waste her hard-earned money; there were several occasions when one or all of them had bumped into him at a Sip popping champagne bottles for a bevy of women. He was lazy and disloyal, and everyone but his wife could see it.

"Why don't we talk about something else?" Zuri said. She held the wine bottle up. "Who needs more wine?" Four glasses shot up. She laughed. "Okay," she said, getting up to make the rounds. "And now someone tell me about some fabulous piece of clothing that they've recently bought—at least that way I can live vicariously through you!'"

There was laughter around the table and Ladun and Lara both started talking at once, while Tami leaned in to the conversation. Adesuwa gave Zuri a grateful look when she topped her glass off. Zuri just smiled and patted her shoulder.

Hours after the girls had left, Zuri washed the dishes and contemplated the different directions the conversation had veered to during the course of the night. They all seemed to be about different things: men, difficult marriages, apartments, and the burden of bills, having a family, the responsibility of having children or having elderly parents. The truth was one thing was at the core of those conversations—Money! She was confounded by how a close group of friends could have such different ideals when it came to handling money.

Even though Adesuwa had spent most of her twenties downplaying her earnings so she didn't seem too independent to potential suitors, she had managed to attract a husband who had no qualms taking advantage of her income and bending it to his will. So even though she earned a decent income, she wasn't financially independent because how she spent her money was dictated by her husband's whims and desires—not hers.

Tami had fewer responsibilities than the others because her parents were wealthy; she lived at home and her business was more of a fun project rather than something that provided an income to survive on. Her lifestyle was dependent on her daddy and boyfriend *du jour*. When Zuri thought about it, she realised that her money conversations with Tami were never really about saving, investing, or business. They were usually geared toward the next spontaneous holiday or what designer shoes to buy. It definitely seemed like Tami was still in La La Land when it came to her finances.

Ladun was a housewife who firmly believed that bank statements were not her business. Bode could worry about that; her job was to show him how to spend it. To her, she fell in line with the common attitude that it was the sole responsibility of a husband or father to worry about family finances. Zuri wondered whether in an uncertain society whether it was prudent for Ladun not to take an active interest in how her bank account got filled every month. Still, Zuri could recall many women had been unable to maintain the lifestyle to which they had become accustomed to because their husband had lost his job, left them for another woman, or worse—had died suddenly with no will and his extended family had kicked them out and taken over the assets because in many African traditions, women weren't allowed to inherit wealth. Bode's parents seemed very refined, but Zuri still wondered if Ladun was right.

And then there was Lara, who earned more than all of the girls for sure. Her bonuses as an oil trader made even Ladun's jaw drop. However, no matter how much money came in, it seemed like there was always one more hurdle to leap that was not necessarily of her own making. Over the years, Zuri had watched her consistently upgrade her family's accommodations, from an apartment in *Iyana Ipaja* to one in *Gbagada* and then the house in Lekki Phase I. They were all properties Lara paid rent on, and, coupled with the university fees she paid for her siblings abroad, Zuri wondered if Lara had any left over for savings or investments. As it was, she wasn't sure even her friend's salary could withstand the financial burden of her family's expenses.

Zuri considered her friends—women who lived very comfortable lives but didn't seem to have a handle on their finances. Their money seemed like it was being pulled in different directions, most of which were not the direction they intended. *What do we want our money to do?* Zuri mused.

She had never really articulated what exactly she wanted the money she earned to do for her. Although she had taken some decent steps towards figuring out where her money was going, she realised now after weeks of her spending diet that she needed a more concrete plan for any of the changes she had made to be sustainable.

SMART MONEY LESSON: TRACK YOUR EXPENSES

Most people don't know where the money they earn goes. What percentage of your income goes to food? Transportation? Clothes? Just like in any successful business where you track the revenue and costs periodically, it is also important to track the expenses in our personal lives. Nigerian women have to become the CFOs of their financial lives and learn to take control of the income they earn now, instead of waiting for their incomes to increase in the future before they learn to manage money.

Some women have no idea how much their lifestyle costs. She may not spend recklessly, but she subconsciously develops a habit of spending—good or bad. If you don't treat the money you earn with respect, it will leave you with no respect. We have to learn to spend with intention by allocating our resources to reflect the lifestyle we want and are able to sustainably afford. This all starts with having a clear idea of where the money is going in the first place. You have to give up the excuses and learn to control money instead of letting money control you.

EXERCISE: TRACK YOUR SPENDING

1. Write down everything you spent your income on in the last month. This will give you good ideas of how you are spending money and help you identify areas to cut or increase.
2. Review your bank statements from the last twelve months.
3. Separate your findings into wants and needs. Limit your wants and prioritise your needs.
4. Identify three to five things to cut each month that would make a significant impact. Review what you are spending on things like your phone calls and food because these are examples of things that are important but we tend to spend on mindlessly. Assess your spending in these areas and set spending limits.
5. Spend on the things you love and cut expenses ruthlessly in the things that don't matter to you.

CHAPTER 4:
DEALING WITH DEBT

This sun is out in full force! Lara thought as she squinted. This was bad, particularly on a weekend when you had to attend an outdoor function in Lagos.

She got out of her BMW and started walking toward the venue. She was slightly annoyed because it had taken her twenty minutes to find parking and the security man at the house she parked next to had demanded five hundred naira. It wasn't that the money was a lot—she certainly could have tipped him at least that much—it was the sense of entitlement that bugged her.

"Madam, you can't park here unless you pay five hundred," he'd said with authority. She'd just rolled her eyes, wound down the window, and paid up because she hadn't had the patience to argue. This man had turned the small patch of land in front of his *oga's* house into a business, taking advantage of the fact that there was a party happening up the road. *The laws of demand and supply, I guess*, she laughed to herself. This was Lagos—everybody had to hustle to make an extra buck.

As she walked toward the party, tiny beads of sweat started to form at her temples; her makeup had already begun to feel like it was melting off her face and it would probably get worse because Banke was having her son's first birthday celebration in the garden of their beautiful Ikoyi home.

As Lara approached the gate and winced at the damage that the bad road was doing to the heel of her Louboutin's, she realised how much she dreaded these children's parties. It was weird because she loved kids and hoped to have some of her own one day, but that was precisely it. She was approaching her mid-thirties and parties like this just reminded her of everything she didn't have yet (a husband and children) and that her proverbial biological clock was ticking.

Two days ago she had absolutely no intention of making an appearance. She had planned to cite an unavoidable work emergency, call Banke after the party to apologise profusely, and send a gift for her son. However, Zuri had called her last night to guilt trip her into coming.

"You can't be serious, Lara! We've known Banke since university and you know how long she's been trying for a boy! It's good to celebrate with people when they are celebrating and mourn with them when they are mourning." Zuri's tone had reminded Lara of her own mother's. "Remember that one day, you'll get married and have a baby too and won't you expect all your friends to be there to celebrate with you?"

An exasperated Lara finally agreed. "Okay, *oh*! I have heard! I'll be there tomorrow."

Zuri wasn't wrong. It was good to celebrate with people when they were celebrating. Lara believed that at her core, plus there was a part of her that felt slightly sorry for the pressure Banke had been under in the last few years to have a boy. However, her sympathy remained slight because as far as she was concerned, the pressure was mostly self-induced. Of course, Banke's obsession with producing a male child was fed by Nigerian society's obsession with boys coupled with a fair amount of pressure from her in-laws, but the fact was the woman had already had three beautiful girls who were happy and healthy before her son had arrived. Some people hadn't even gotten married nor had the opportunity to have a child, so it was a bit selfish for Banke to expect her sympathy. Banke was also one of those annoying women that started almost every sentence with, 'My husband said' or 'You won't understand because you don't have kids.' The more Lara thought about previous conversations she had engaged in with Banke, the more irritable her mood became.

She passed through security, checked her name off the guest list, and navigated her way through to Banke's garden. Their backyard had been transformed into some sort of kiddie's wonderland. She recognised some characters from a cartoon she was sure she grew up watching but couldn't quite place the name. There was a little boy and lots of animals and the place looked like an actual forest. As she walked by a wooden sign that said *Wild Jungle Party Starts Here...Rumble in the Jungle* it hit her. It was The Jungle Book! *How clever*, Lara thought. As she approached the kids' eating area, which was surrounded by a mix of large palm trees and coconut trees, she couldn't help but marvel at how realistic the jungle looked—they must have spent a fortune on décor.

"Hi Banke, where's the birthday boy?" Lara air-kissed her friend on both cheeks and gave her a faux hug.

"He's having the time of his life in the playpen with the other kids his age. It's such a pity he's not old enough to play in the tree house with the older kids. You know, it took the carpenters two whole days to erect that thing," Banke replied, with a smug, self-satisfied look.

As she walked toward the adult section to find Zuri, Lara looked up at the beautifully constructed tree house, which had actual vines and leaves hanging from them. There was also a spectacular waterfall, flanked by rocks on each side and complete with fun plastic flamingos bobbing in the water. Lara took it all in, amused. She wasn't sure why she even bothered being surprised anymore. This was Lagos, where almost everything was a large-scale production including a one-year-old's birthday party. The extravaganzas were never about the child though. They were really about the parents and their "celebration of life". A party like this would surely have set them back a few million naira.

She spotted Zuri and tried to wave to catch her attention but she was deep in conversation with another woman. As she got closer to their table she realised the girl was Chinasa, who Lara despised. It wasn't because she had done anything to her directly—she just hated everything the girl stood for. She was a fairly young fashionista who had found a way to ingratiate herself into every social stratum in Lagos, regardless of age; there were forty-year-old guys she was besties with! Even Lara had to admit that, she had the whole innocent, I'm-such-a-sweet-girl act down pat. The thing was, Lara had heard some rather unsavoury things come out of the girl's mouth about others, it was a wonder that more people didn't see through her.

She had once mentioned to Lara at another party that a famous actress she was working with was broke, couldn't afford her services, was always begging for freebies, was sleeping around

Lagos for money and how she couldn't stand her because she lacked morals. The following week on Instagram Lara spotted an emotional post the actress put up of Chinasa, saying how she was such an amazing person who was so selfless and loyal. It made Lara sick to her stomach. She wondered what the rat was telling Zuri now.

"Yaaay! Lara you made it," Zuri said as she stood up to hug her.

"What's wrong with you, *sef*? I told you I was coming, *na*," Lara laughed.

"Hey sis," said Chinasa, sounding rather excited.

"Hey," Lara responded with a forced smile. She looked at Zuri. "Can you come with me to find the bathroom? The heat is destroying my makeup, I need to go and touch up, so I'm not out here looking crazy."

"Haaahaa, you look fine, *jo!*" Zuri replied. "I'll show you where it is. Chinasa we'll be back soon, okay?"

They both stood in the guest bathroom in front of the mirror, examining their faces. Lara reached for her House of Tara compact and dabbed her T-zone to remove any traces of oil while Zuri retouched her House of Tara *Arese* Lipstick.

"What was that Chinasa girl saying to you?" Lara asked. "You know she is quite the gossip, be careful what you say to her. She's one of those people you don't have to even tell actual gist to, they can twist even the most mundane piece of information and then *carry your matter* like a town crier."

Zuri laughed. "It's funny! She was actually saying the vilest things about Banke. I can't lie—I wanted to hear the gist but at the same time it made me uncomfortable because we are still in the woman's house for God's sake."

"Vile? how so? *Abeg*, spill! What did she say?" Lara laughed. "Even me, I want to hear."

"Basically she was saying that Banke and Femi can never afford the lavish parties they've become known for."

"They are loaded, *now*! Femi has been running a lucrative oil and gas business for years. What is that small rat on about?" Lara scoffed.

"Ha! The girl said it took Banke a year to finish paying off all the vendors from her third child's birthday party two years ago."

"Zuri *abeg*, stop that joke! Which Lagos vendors will let someone owe them for one year and not disgrace them?" Lara said as she rolled her eyes.

"Girrrl, that's what I said too, *oh,* but Chinasa claims that Banke had paid substantial deposits before the party and just stopped picking up their calls after the party was done. Apparently it didn't become a big scandal because of their family name and the vendors didn't want to spoil the prospect of future business with Banke, seeing as she's known for throwing lavish parties."

"That's so bizarre! I wonder if there's any truth to it."

"That wasn't all, *oh*! She said Banke owed several Nigerian designers around Lagos for clothes they had made for her and she had yet to pay for. She said combined the debt she had racked up was in the millions." Zuri clapped her hands dramatically. "Anyway please don't repeat this—I'm tired of this Lagos, only God knows if any of it is true and I'm pretty sure we are not the only ones that have heard this gist. Let's go back out to the party."

Lara nodded. All this at a one-year-old's birthday party. It was mind boggling.

***

As she and Lara approached their table, Zuri noticed that a few guys had joined Chinasa and they were deep in discussion.

"See you. It's all bank funded, their entire lifestyle," said Tunji, one of Femi's friends.

"Is it just that? Does he pay his staff? He doesn't! Meanwhile they'll be throwing a party that cost millions," said a guy Zuri couldn't quite place.

Chinasa was smiling coquettishly. "Hmmm *egbon*, are you sure? Banke just asked me to style her for December because she has so many events to attend. Do you think I should take the job? Because I'm really busy in December, you know since that Bella Naija article the whole world wants me to style them and I'm overwhelmed. I would hate to give up other jobs for her and not get paid. Advise me? What do you think I should do?"

Zuri observed Chinasa in appalled awe. Lara was right—this girl had the whole *I'm so innocent* routine down pat. The looks she threw at Tunji and his friend like a damsel in distress were at odds with the fact that she had just said some pretty nasty things about Banke. It was obvious that Chinasa had led everyone down the path of discussing the couple's supposed money woes.

On her drive home later that evening, Zuri reflected on everything she had heard that day. The combination of stories about Banke and Femi and their *gbese* made her feel, well, *some type of way*. That Chinasa girl was mean-spirited; she was surprised she hadn't really noticed that about her before but she couldn't imagine what she had to gain from spreading these stories and inciting even more malicious ones. It didn't even matter if they were true or not. Banke had invited her to her son's birthday because she thought she was so sweet. *It's funny,* Zuri thought, *how you never know what people really think of you or what they were capable of saying about you even under your own roof.* Banke would have a fit if she ever heard.

As her cab drove through the gates of her apartment building, Zuri contemplated her own money situation. She looked up at the balconies of her neighbours and wondered if there were rumours already circulating about her inability to pay the service charge. Mr Okeke would have undoubtedly complained about her to at least one or two other residents—and the Lagos gist mill would have new fodder to grind. Zuri began checking her email as she walked up the stairs to her flat.

There was a very polite email from Nneka, the retail manager at Zazaii, reminding her that she had an eighty-thousand-naira balance to pay at the end of the month and an extra late fee of fifteen percent would be added to the agreed two percent credit fee if payment was not made by the thirtieth of the month.
Zuri sat on her bed and reread the email and examined the invoice

Nneka had sent. Zazaii had a credit policy for their loyal high-end customers, which she enjoyed. It was usually for clients who worked at banks, whose debt could be deducted directly from their salaries at the end of the month, but they charged an additional two percent premium and customers were expected to pay within thirty days.

At this point it occurred to Zuri that she had not fully accounted for her total debt. She had only been stressed about the immediate threats; she had obsessively thought about little else other than Mr Okeke and how she could possibly pay him in good time. She had completely forgotten about the trickle debt that was adding up to another river. Sixty thousand for two *aṣo-ebi* she had collected on credit. Seventy thousand for some Indian hair that a friend had brought from the US. This was becoming a mess, even though she had made several changes to her spending in the last few weeks. She needed to confront her debt in its entirety and formulate a strategy to beat it down.

A plan began to form in her mind. It was drastic but simple and, more importantly, it would be effective.

She made a list of all her debts—an amount and the name of the person or business she owed. The total came to one point one-two million. It was not a small amount but consolidating it made it less scary.

Then she prioritised the debts according to their urgency. Mr Okeke was at the top of the list. She needed a place to live. She set a schedule for how long it would take to pay off each debt—placing a realistic timeline for when she could afford to pay off each loan. She didn't want to make the timelines too comfortable but she knew they had to be paid off as quickly as possible so she could be debt free.

Next? Raising money to clear her debts. She had already been able to save two hundred and ten thousand from the previous month but that still left a substantial amount of the debt to clear. She earned six hundred thousand naira so she decided she could squeeze out another two hundred and twenty thousand from her salary this month to pay Mr Okeke in full. Paying in instalments would only drag the misery out longer since the next bill for service charge was already looming.

Tami had told her about a shopping consignment outfit called Luxury Concierge which could help her offload her designer bags fairly quickly if they were in decent condition. She called them and set up a meeting, so their staff could inspect and value the bags to set a realistic selling price. One of the co-founders, Mariah, had spoken with her on the phone had told her that if everything went well they could sell the bags for as much as four hundred thousand each in about ten days, because Chanel and Alexander McQueen were in high demand.

She would sell the car; it was costing her too much money just to maintain it. It would have been easier to buy and manage a brand new Toyota, but at the time, the sweet bonus she got when she started her job at Richmond made it almost impossible to turn down the terrific offer she was getting from a friend of a friend who had to sell the car because he was moving abroad.
A thirty-minute conversation later, Zuri had persuaded her

mechanic to put her car on the market and to recoup the two hundred thousand she owed him from the profits of the sale. He would get a five percent commission for assisting her with selling the car. She had also convinced Tami to pick her up for work for a while. Tami had grumbled but Zuri knew she could always rely on her in times like this. She knew it wasn't a sustainable solution but it would have to do for now.

She placed a long overdue phone call to Dr Emeka. He told her the fibroids weren't aggressive and she had some time to consider her treatment options, which included just leaving them alone if they weren't growing; apparently many women her age opted to have babies even with the fibroids, with the choice to take them out after delivery. All the options terrified her, but she felt better knowing she had a clearer plan to address her healthcare issues.

SMART MONEY LESSON: SLAY YOUR DEBT

Debt can be a useful tool to attain financial success but how you use it matters. Wealthy people use debt as a tool to leverage their investments and grow their cash flow, but poor people use debt to buy things that make rich people richer. Only borrow to acquire an asset that will appreciate in value.

People with bad debt habits will typically go into debt buying things their income cannot support. They will borrow money to purchase big-ticket items that don't appreciate in value and most likely can't cover the cost of the debt over time.

EXERCISE: UNDERSTAND YOUR DEBT AND DEAL WITH IT

1. Acknowledge the total amount of your debt by making a list.
2. Set a repayment schedule that includes how much you owe each person or institution.
3. Prioritise your debts. Decide which ones are most important. This depends on your particular situation—you could slay the largest debt first to give you more confidence that the rest are manageable, or you could decide it is best to start with the debt charged with the highest interest rate, so the debt does not increase. Otherwise, it's best to pay the one with the most imminent wahala (in Zuri's case her landlord was hounding her and further non-payment could have led to eviction).
4. Set deadlines for each loan. There should be an estimate of how long it is going to take you to pay off each debt.
5. Decide how you plan to raise the money to pay. For example, deciding to cut your outflow to create room in your budget every month towards paying down your debt, finding another source of income or selling off valuable items you don't necessarily need are all options to consider.
6. Think about the triggers that led you into debt in the first place and try to eliminate them. There's no point getting out of debt only to dive back in.

CHAPTER 5:
SURVIVING EMERGENCIES

Zuri stirred as she heard her phone ringing. She had heard it ring a few times already but she thought she was dreaming. As the phone stopped buzzing she reached for it to look at the time. It was 4:25 a.m.! Who could be calling at this ungodly hour? She tapped the green button on her iPhone that indicated she had six missed calls. It was Aunty Uwa, her mother's sister in Benin.

Wow! This woman couldn't be serious! Actually, why am I even surprised? Zuri thought. Her "Bini" relatives were the champions of doing this—calling people early in the morning or better still showing up at your front door as early as 6:00 a.m. This was apparently to indicate how important the issue they wanted to discuss was but the truth was, it was usually not *that* important. Zuri was used to Aunty Uwa's random phone calls early in the morning for prayers. However, in reality it was unsolicited advice about how Zuri needed to find a husband and settle down so she could make her mother proud.

"Do you think she's happy tying *gele* every weekend to attend other people's children's wedding? Don't you want her to dance as mother of the bride too? All this career nonsense won't keep you warm at night *oh*. *Abi* you don't want children? Time is going, *oh*, and you are not getting any younger. Look at your cousin, Nekpen. She's only twenty-five and she already has three children," she would say.

Her lectures would go on for at least an hour. She suspected it was her mother that put Aunty Uwa up to these antics, so it wouldn't look like she was putting pressure on her directly. The early morning phone calls had stopped for a while but now this! *How can she be calling me at four thirty in the morning?* Zuri fumed. *How was this okay? Even for Aunty Uwa this was ridiculously early; she had never called before 6:00 a.m. before! When nobody died? HAAA! What if somebody died?* Zuri panicked.

"Calm down!" she chided herself out loud. "This is Aunty Uwa we are talking about! Nothing serious has happened. She's probably just in her feelings. I better get up and shower first; I can call her while I'm getting dressed for work, before she makes me late."

Zuri dialled Aunty Uwa's number and put the phone on speaker as she smoothed her shea and cocoa butter cream over her skin.

Aunty Uwa picked up after the first ring.

"Hello Aunty! Good morning," Zuri said.

"Zuri I've been calling you since morning! Why didn't you pick up?"

"Sorry Aunty, I was sleeping," Zuri said, needling her aunt just a bit.

"What kind of foolish sleep is that? If I call you six times, don't you know it's important?" Aunty Uwa yelled angrily, followed by some Bini words Zuri did not understand.

"I'm sorry, Aunty." *Not really.* "It won't happen again. Please tell me what happened."

"It's your mother, *oh*!" said Aunty Uwa.

"My mum? What happened? Is she okay?!" Zuri cried out, putting her hands over her mouth.

"Her house caught fire last night!" Aunty Uwa shouted.

"Oh my God! Oh my God! Is Mummy okay? Please tell me she's okay!" Zuri began to cry.

"Thank God for the neighbour's security that saw it in time. She's fine—a little shaken up because she inhaled some smoke, but the doctors say she's going to be okay. The house is thankfully not completely damaged—only the living room and guest room were affected."

Zuri collapsed in relief. "How did this even happen?"

"The air conditioner caught fire in the guest room downstairs. It spread a little to the living room but they were able to stop it before it destroyed the rest of the house. Your mummy is fine, don't worry. She's going to stay at my house for now. she's finally sleeping now, so I took her phone so people will not disturb her. You can call her later on. You'll come to Benin this weekend, *abi*?" She said in a tone that indicated it was an instruction, not a suggestion.

"Yes ma, I will come. Thank you for letting me know and for looking after Mummy," Zuri said.

As she ended the conversation with her aunt and tried to focus on getting ready to go to work, she couldn't help but worry about her mother. When Zuri's dad died of cancer eight years ago, her mother continued to live in Benin by herself. As the only one left in Nigeria, Zuri was the only one who saw her regularly. She was sure Aunty Uwa would have called her brothers already, but she sent them both an email to notify them of the situation.

***

She had been in the office since 7:30 a.m. There had been no traffic, which was quite strange for a Wednesday morning in Lagos. Still she wasn't being very productive. She had been staring listlessly at quarterly reports for hours but her mind was with her mum in Benin. The news of the fire had really scared her. She shuddered to think about what could have happened if they hadn't stopped it in time. The fire service in Lagos wasn't very efficient, not to talk of Benin. She actually wasn't even sure if there was a fire service there.

"Hey Zuri, Mr Tunde said to tell everyone we are having a meeting in the conference room at 11:00 a.m.," Sandra said as she walked past Zuri's desk.

"*Ah ah.* Why? It's Wednesday—why would we have an all staff meeting on Wednesday? Did something happen?"

Sandra shrugged. "That's what he said, but he's being very cryptic about it. He won't tell anyone what it's regarding. *Biko*, just help me pass on the message to the people in your department."

A little before eleven, Zuri walked into the conference room behind a stream of other staff. She wondered what this impromptu meeting could be about. As she found a seat next to Obiangeli from accounting, she searched the faces of the senior partners for answers. They all looked grim; none of them were smiling, and even the ones who were usually friendly, like Mr Obi, were acting a little weird. She caught his eye and smiled but he looked away and as she watched the senior partners exchange looks of pity, she sensed that there was something terribly wrong.

Father Lord, I can't handle any more bad news today, Zuri thought as she looked around the room. People were whispering to themselves and drawing their own conclusions as to what could have happened.

"They are letting people go, in case you were wondering," Obiangeli said matter-of-factly.

"Really?" *Is she serious?! Now?!* "How do you know? Who told you?" Zuri said.

"No one has to tell me. I work in the finance department! When there is more money going out than there is coming in and we can't pay our suppliers on time, it's not rocket science they have to restructure."

Zuri began to panic. *Sales had been slow but not slow enough for them to start sacking people,* na? Just last week Alex from procurement had been complaining about how a combination of the naira devaluation and the capital controls put in place by the Central Bank of Nigeria was making it much more expensive for the company to import some of the materials they needed to complete several of their real estate projects.

She wondered what this meant for her. Even though she had stepped up her game in the last few weeks, she was still on probation with Mr Tunde. She said a silent prayer and crossed her fingers.

As Mr Tunde walked into the room, people gradually got quieter. The tension could be cut with a knife. Mr Tunde cleared his throat and then made his announcement.

The company was letting twenty-five people go.

A mixture of market forces, CBN policy and new banking regulation had forced the company into a precarious position, and the company needed to make some tough decisions in order to survive, Mr Tunde explained. The company needed to tighten its belt.

He began to read the names. The room was dead silent. He finished, thanked everyone and left. Then it hit her. Mr Tunde had finished reading and hadn't said her name. Was this a long drawn out prank or a narrow escape? In that moment, she made a vow to work harder and add value to the company. She was so grateful for this second chance. Today was truly a day of narrow escapes; first the fire, then this. As she turned to Obiangeli to say as much, she noticed she was crying. Zuri realised that because she was so nervous about her own name being called, she hadn't realised Obiangeli's name was on the list.

"Are you going to be okay?" Zuri asked as she patted the woman's back.

She let out a muffled "I'm fine!" as she rushed out of the conference room.

Zuri followed her to the ladies' room. She stood there quietly as she watched Obiangeli wash her face in the bathroom sink.

"I've given this company my best in the last two years. I've worked late nights and I'm one of the first to get in every morning. I just can't understand why I deserve to get sacked," Obiangeli cried. "It's just not fair."

"I'm so sorry Obiangeli! I'm really sorry. Is there anything I can do to help?" Zuri said, trying to comfort her.

Obiangeli stared at her. "Is there anything you can do to help?" she said with more than a hint of derision. "I just lost my job—my family's only source of income—and I have three children who depend on me to feed them and pay school fees. It took me almost a year of job hunting to get this position, so I know it won't be easy to find another one. My family is basically in trouble because it's not like this salary was fantastic to begin with. It's a struggle to make ends meet every month so we don't even have any substantial savings. So what can you do for me, Princess Zuri? Absolutely nothing! I would appreciate it if you left me alone."

Zuri's face burned with embarrassment. "I'm really sorry," she mumbled before leaving the bathroom.

She didn't have time to think about Obiangeli's stinging comments though, because Sandra told her that Mr Tunde wanted to see her in his office. Again.

She had been right in the middle of searching for cheap flights to Benin. She could barely afford the return ticket given her money situation but travelling by road would be a bad idea at this time of the year. The roads were extremely bad and the rainy season would have made it even worse. Plus, she would spend most of the time on the road instead of maximising the time spent commiserating with her mother. Zuri had finally spoken to her and more than anything, she was worried about not having enough funds to repair the damage to the house.

"Did he say why?" Zuri asked.

Sandra laughed. "Does he ever say why? Just go, *jo!* He is waiting for you."

As Zuri walked to Mr Tunde's office, she wondered if he was going to sack her privately. It didn't make any sense that they would fire a rule-follower like Obiangeli and not fire Zuri who broke the rules often, and had not exactly been employee of the year for quite some time now.

She said a quick prayer as she knocked on Mr Tunde's door.

"Zuri, come in. Take a seat, I'd like to have a word," Mr Tunde said. "Let me just get straight to the point. You realise that because you are on probation you should have been fired today, right?"

Zuri nodded.

"We decided to give you a second chance because you seem to have stepped up your game since our talk," Mr Tunde said with a smile. "However, more importantly, given the challenges the company is experiencing, we need your particular skill-set but you are going to have to really apply yourself because this is a huge responsibility. Are you up for it?"

Zuri nodded again. "Yes, of course I am. Thank you, sir. I promise not to let you down. Thank you so much."

"I hope so," Mr Tunde said sternly. "Anyway, let's get down to business. We've been in talks with a private equity firm called Zuma Capital. Have you heard of them?"

"The name sounds vaguely familiar, sir, but I'll do my research right after this meeting," Zuri said quickly, hoping not to irritate him.

"That's fine," Mr Tunde said. "They are an up-and-coming private equity firm based in Lagos. They only started about eight years ago but they've been responsible for at least four major deals, which includes their most recent acquisition, the transportation company SMBD. Anyway, they haven't done any major real estate deals yet, so we are in negotiations with them to come in as co-investors and take an equity stake in some of our unfinished real estate developments. They usually don't do deals less than ten million dollars, but thankfully they seem interested in starting our working relationship with baby steps. Instead of acquiring the company, they are looking at investing in each project separately and getting their returns from sales. However, they'd like to see how viable each project is. We have a meeting with them first thing in the morning, so I'm going to need you to work with all the departments to provide a valuation, projected cash flows, and a sales strategy. I don't care if you have to work all night but I'm going to need you to put the documents together and prepare a presentation that will blow their minds tomorrow."

"Not a problem, sir," Zuri said, trying to sound as upbeat and ready as she could.

"You can go ahead and start—I don't need to tell you how important this transaction is."

"I really appreciate this opportunity," Zuri replied. "I'll get started right away."

"Zuri," Mr Tunde said abruptly, as she reached the door. "I know this is last-minute but you know these properties more than most people at this office so I trust you can do this. You just need to focus. You've pitched them to clients before—you just need to work the numbers and bring your A-game tomorrow."

"I'll be ready."

* * *

It was 1:00 a.m. and Zuri looked at all the pieces of paper strewn across her sofa and on the rug beneath. They were evidence of all the work she had put into making this presentation solid. After hours of analysis, back and forth phone calls to Kachukwu and Alice (who worked in financial control and operations, respectively) to verify information and get feedback on her approach, she finally felt prepared. It was important to her to not just impress the potential investors but also prove to Mr Tunde and the other senior partners that she was a valuable part of the company and they hadn't made a mistake keeping her on.

As she struggled to put on her pyjamas and get into bed, she reflected on her day and the financial consequences she would have ultimately had to face if her mother's house had burnt down completely or she had lost her job. She was still months away from repaying all her debts and she definitely didn't have enough in her account to look after herself in the event that she lost her job. She knew today she had dodged several bullets, but she also knew that next time, she might not be so lucky.

SMART MONEY LESSON: BUILD AN EMERGENCY FUND

We live in a very superstitious society. So, even when we hear the terrible stories of people losing their jobs, or women losing the bread winners of their households suddenly, then forced into relative pennilessness because they can no longer afford their rent and have to beg friends and family for money to pay the children's school fees, we think 'God forbid not me'. Sometimes, though, bad things happen to good people. So instead of worrying without action, we need to plan for emergencies.

A smart woman doesn't wait for financial surprises; she systematically saves toward her emergency fund because she knows that this is the foundation of her financial journey. The cushion that acts as a financial safety net, so before you splurge make sure you have at least six to nine months of living expenses saved up for emergencies. An emergency fund is not there to make you money but to act as a financial cushion that protects your long term investments from short term unexpected expenses.

EXERCISE: BUILD AN EMERGENCY FUND

1. Calculate how much you would need to survive if you lost your job or income from your business. What do your living expenses add up to each month? Multiply that by six or nine months. Factor in things like rent and utilities.
2. Strictly define emergencies. Your car breaking down or having to pay an unexpected hospital bill qualify as emergencies. A phone upgrade, an impromptu trip to Dubai or those YSL pumps on sale do not.
3. Shore up your emergency fund with windfalls like cash gifts, bonuses or extra work done. i.e. when you get money you were not expecting, commit to using a percentage (at least 20%) of it to top up your emergency fund.
4. Don't put it in a risky asset class, i.e. stocks. It is not there to make you money.
5. The most important elements of an emergency fund are liquidity and safety, not return, so do not take risks to earn more or sacrifice liquidity.
6. Look for high interest savings accounts or money market accounts that preserve your capital and give you a reasonable return.

CHAPTER 6:
MONEY GOALS

The rain had caused immense traffic. She was fifteen minutes late for the meeting and even though she had texted Mr Tunde twenty minutes ago to explain the reasons for the delay, she knew he wouldn't be pleased and she would probably be fired if her presentation wasn't convincing enough.

"I'm so sorry I'm late," Zuri said as she looked apologetically at the delegation from Zuma Capital. There were three of them: a woman, Folake, and two men, Tsola, and Ebuka. She had done as much research as she could on the three of them last night.

Folake was a very impressive young woman. She looked to be in her mid-thirties, had an MBA from Harvard and had started her career at Morgan Stanley as an analyst, worked at The Abraaj Group as an investor before she joined Zuma Capital as a junior partner.

Ebuka was in his forties, married with three children, and had worked at Goldman Sachs for eighteen years before he left to start Zuma Capital with Tsola.

Tsola Preware. He was thirty-eight, went to Cambridge then Stanford, had worked in several investment banks including Goldman Sachs before he moved to Nigeria to work for the biggest indigenous private equity firm, where he became notorious for structuring and executing some of the biggest deals the company had been part of in the last five years. He was a bit of a legend in the finance community. Zuri had watched several interviews of him on CNBC Africa and he exuded a brash confidence that bordered on cocky. She found him very attractive. He wasn't handsome in a pretty boy way, though; he was good-looking, yes, but it was his swag and the way he carried himself and spoke as though he knew he was always the smartest person in the room. Intimidating, but sexy.

As Zuri looked up from trying to get the projector to work so she could start her presentation without any further delays she saw him staring at her with an impatient look on his face. Her heart sank. He thought she was incompetent before she had even begun.

"We would appreciate it if you could hurry up," Tsola said coldly. "We have several meetings to get to and we are already twenty minutes behind as it is."

"I'm so sorry, sir. Let's begin," Zuri said.

Zuri could feel Tsola watching her as she walked them through the features of the two developments Richmond needed capital to complete. She tried to sound upbeat and confident but she knew she mostly sounded nervous.

* * *

Tsola watched Zuri's presentation. She hid it well, but he could tell she was nervous; she smoothed the non-existent wrinkles in her skirts just a bit too often.
Still, there was something in her that made him want to challenge and unsettle her even more.

Maybe it was the fact that she looked like the sort of girl who usually got away with a lot because of the effect she had on men. She was hot but this was a business meeting and she had already irritated him with her tardiness. He had three meetings after this and a flight to catch at 6:00 p.m. He wasn't going to let anything slide. Women like her had to learn to use their brains and not depend on their good looks.

"Listen madam, enough with the features, we get it!" Tsola interrupted. "I have three more meetings after this and a flight to catch at six. Let's get to the important stuff—the numbers. Have you done an independent valuation of each development? What have been your profit margins on the sale of flats in that area historically? What kind of rental income can we expect if we decide to co-invest?"

"Zuri, what Tsola is trying to say is that we are concerned that the return on investment on this deal might be a lot smaller than we are used to," Folake interjected with a look at Tsola.

* * *

Zuri was irritated, but tried not to show it. She hated it when someone who was clearly older than her referred to her as *madam*. He obviously meant to be condescending but she knew she had to keep her cool and be professional. So, she looked at Tsola and smiled. *Bring it on.*

It was clear he thought she was just a pretty face with no in-depth understanding of the deal structure but she had done her research and even called a few of her friends in the private equity space—this was a good deal for Zuma Capital. They had several deals in Nigeria that would pay out in the long-term but needed to be invested in some projects that could also provide them with some liquidity in the short-term.

"I apologise, Mr. Preware, I was only trying to familiarise you and your team with the features of the development so you could get an understanding of our USP and put the valuations in context. I'll skip right to the details."

As Zuri talked through her slides, she explained the more than decent profit margins that were expected from the sale of ten of the flats and the rental income from the five-year lease they were negotiating with one of the largest telecoms firms.

"As you can see, these will both be high revenue-generating projects upon completion. Unfortunately, between the currency crisis, falling oil prices, and the general turmoil in the Nigerian economy, the cost of both projects shot up by more than thirty percent and without funding from the bank or additional funding from our international investors, who want to limit their exposure to the Nigerian market, at the moment it's proved very difficult to complete either development.

"I understand that Zuma is usually interested in much larger deals, but this could present two opportunities for you. For starters, it will provide you with some liquidity in the short-term because, unlike other real estate development deals that haven't even broken ground, we are eighty percent to completion, so the revenues from our rental incomes will start rolling in almost immediately. The other upside is the capital appreciation on the units that we don't sell. The ROI on this deal is decent, and investing in this smaller project can act as a test case—working with us on these relatively short-term projects will be an indication of whether you should buy the group or not."

"Uhm, thank you, Zuri," Mr Tunde said. "Ebuka, what are your thoughts?"

"Well, the young lady has made quite a compelling case," Ebuka said with a wry smile. "Obviously, like Folake said, there are concerns as to whether the expected returns are worth our while or not, but give us the weekend to discuss it and we'll get back to you early next week with a decision and hopefully a term sheet." He winked at Zuri.

As Mr Tunde ushered the Zuma capital team out of the office, she caught Tsola staring at her, looking bemused. She sensed that he wanted to say something but then he looked away as though he had changed his mind. There was something about him that made her uncomfortable. She couldn't decide if it was his aura or the fact that he was just so damn confident.

When Mr Tunde came back in, Zuri couldn't quite read the expression on his face.

"Well," he said finally. "I guess that went alright. Now we wait to hear back. I hate this part."

"I'm sorry," Zuri said. "Maybe if I had given a better presentation, they would've given us an answer right away."

Mr Tunde shook his head. "I asked you to step up your game, Zuri, and you did. I'm actually rather pleased with how well it all came together, especially considering the short time frame."

"Thank you," Zuri said, though she knew she wouldn't be able to feel truly great about it until Zuma had gotten back to them with a yes. Later, Zuri found herself at the airport, just in time to hear that her flight to Benin had been delayed. She had done her best to get to the airport early, so she could avoid the beast that was Lagos traffic especially on a Friday, the traffic wasn't as bad as expected because she got to the airport with an hour to spare before boarding started, she was hopeful that her journey to Benin would be smooth and without the usual hiccups. Apparently not.

She began to put her things together so she could walk the length of the departure lounge and exercise her now numb legs, then she spotted a familiar face walking in her direction. For a second, she couldn't place him, but as the man drew nearer and his face came into focus, she realised it was Tsola. He was no longer wearing his sharp designer suit from their meeting earlier this morning, but it was definitely him. Instead, he wore a white, well-tailored traditional outfit that had a slim fit and displayed his lean swimmer's shoulders and all six-foot one of him nicely.

She avoided his gaze and attempted to feign ignorance of his presence as she walked past.

"Hello again, madam."

No such luck, she thought. "Hello, sir," Zuri said, forcing a smile.

"Where are you off to? Abuja?" Tsola asked.

"No, I'm going to Benin but the flight has been delayed for another hour."

"Oh! I'm on the same flight." Tsola smiled. "What's happening in Benin? Visiting family? Or is this a work related trip?"

"Family. I'm going to visit my mum. There was a fire and her home has been damaged."

"Wow! I'm so sorry to hear that. Is she okay?" Tsola said.

"She's fine, thankfully she got out of the house in time, so she wasn't injured, just some smoke inhalation but the doctor says she'll be okay."

Tsola nodded. There was an awkward silence.

Zuri moved to say her goodbyes.

Then Tsola said suddenly, "You should come and sit with me in the lounge upstairs. The chairs up there are much more comfortable. Besides," he added with a slightly amused smile, "I don't bite."

There was a part of Zuri that couldn't imagine what she would be talking for an hour to Tsola about, but she still felt numb from the waist down after sitting on the uncomfortable metal seats and at this point the prospect of sitting in the air-conditioned lounge with leather chairs was rather enticing.

"Great!" she said trying to sound unbothered. Before she could say anything else Tsola took her tiny suitcase from her as they walked up the stairs to the lounge.

Zuri smiled at this unexpected gesture. Some Nigerian men didn't really do the whole "gentleman" thing. She couldn't remember the last time a man had helped her with her bags or opened a door for her, especially not someone that could be categorised as a "Lagos big boy". It was refreshing.

As they settled into their seats in a little corner of the lounge, he asked her about her family, about work. He was surprisingly easy to talk to. There were no uncomfortable silences and he seemed genuinely interested in everything she had to say, including the mundane stuff. He seemed like a completely different person from the man who had confronted her in the meeting earlier that day.

"So did you grow up in Benin?" Tsola said.

"Yes *oh*, I'm a *Bini* girl through and through, even though I can't speak the language." Zuri laughed.

"That's disappointing. I think every Nigerian should speak at least one native language, otherwise our culture will be lost. I speak four Nigerian languages—Itsekiri, Yoruba, Hausa and Igbo. They come in handy when you are trying to close deals." He winked.

"Four Nigerian languages? Wow! Way to shame me," Zuri laughed.

"So what does your dad have to say about you not able to speak *Bini*?" Tsola said.

"Not much. He died several years ago," she said and her smile dimmed a little.

"Oh I'm sorry to hear that," Tsola said. "So who looks after your mum in Benin? Who is going to help her sort out the whole issue of the house? Do you have insurance?"

"Insurance, *ke*?" Zuri said, laughing.

"Yes, insurance to cover the damage on her house."

Zuri felt a little defensive. "Uhm, no. I didn't even think of that. Besides insurance is a waste of money in this part of the world, they don't pay, or they won't pay anything significant."

"That's a myth!" Tsola said. "If you are on the right insurance plan and pay your premiums regularly, insurance is a great way to protect your assets. I think it's an excuse that most Nigerians give themselves for not wanting to pay that premium when times are good. We are quite a superstitious society, so we never like to think about what if my house burns down or my car has an accident? The mentality is usually 'God forbid, it won't happen to me'," Tsola laughed. "But the reality is sometimes bad things happen to good people. At least if you had some insurance it would help to cover some of the costs even if it's not all of it. So how are you going to cover the cost of repairing the damage?"

"I have no idea. My plan was to go to Benin, get someone to assess the damage, and then see what my brothers and I can contribute towards it," Zuri said. "More my brothers because I'm extremely broke at the moment." She laughed, slightly embarrassed that she had said that out loud.

"*Fine girl* like you, broke? How so?" Tsola teased.

Zuri told him about her mounting debt, inability to pay her service charge, the rent that was looming, her issues with her car, her challenges at work, and her fear that she could lose her job at any minute. She was self-conscious because he was practically a stranger and she didn't want him to think she was the type of Nigerian girl who was unloading all her problems before she asked for a hand out. When she finished speaking though, she felt... better. This was the first time she had unburdened herself since her money *wahala* had started.

***

Tsola observed her absentmindedly as she relayed the story of how she almost lost her job and all her money problems. She had a strange effect on him and he couldn't quite place a finger on why. She was attractive, yes; not conventionally beautiful, but definitely pretty. Beyond that she was something more.

He founded her brand of awkwardness sexy. He usually wasn't talkative but there was something about this girl that made him want to tell her his life story, his goals, fears, his dreams and hear hers. She was intelligent and witty but seemed to lack direction. She was one of those people who just allowed life to happen to them because she obviously didn't have a plan. He wanted to laugh at what she considered money problems but he thought the best of it, she was obviously in a vulnerable place in her life and quite sensitive about it.

There was a part of him that wanted to shake her and tell her to *wake the hell up*! She was focused on the wrong things. She was weighing herself down with the problems instead of focusing on the possible solutions. She was brilliant but she wasn't maximising her earning potential. The debt she was moaning about was inconsequential in the grand scheme of things if she played her cards right. Earlier that day, he had watched her sway him and his partners in a new direction in that conference room. His first impression of her had been wrong. She had a unique perspective and a power of persuasion that was rare in someone so young. She could certainly be putting her sales skills to better use instead of sitting in a cubicle crunching numbers all day.

"What do you want?" Tsola said.

"What do I want? I... I don't know."
"You must have some idea. Clearly, you're intelligent and witty but you lack direction. You're one of those people who just allow life happen because you don't have a plan. You need to wake up—you're focused on the wrong things."

Zuri looked at him in confusion. "I am?"

"Yes. You're focusing on your problems, not the possible solutions. I'll admit, when I met you earlier today, I made some stupid assumptions because you are good-looking, but you have since proven me wrong. You have a unique perspective and a power of persuasion that is rare in someone so young, but you're squandering it. You're not putting it to good use and you are yet to understand money or how it works. First, you've got to figure out what you want."

The question made her uncomfortable. Luckily, she was saved when they announced that the flight was ready to board and they could begin getting on the plane. But of course Tsola made sure that his seat was right next to hers, and once they were sitting, he looked at her expectantly, still waiting her answer to his question.

"What do I want from you?" Zuri asked hesitantly as her mind wandered back to their conversation.

"No, from life." Tsola laughed. "What do you want from life?"

Zuri wasn't quite sure where all this was going. "Uhm, I don't know? I guess I want what every normal person wants?" Zuri said hesitantly.

"Like what?" Tsola probed. "And what does *normal* even mean? Trust me—what I want out of life is probably different from what you want out of life! The problem is most people focus on earning a paycheque so they can survive and not focus enough on articulating what they want the money they earn to do for them."

Zuri stared at him blankly. "I don't understand; everyone wants to ball, *na*? We want to live in fancy houses, fly first class, shop for all the bags and shoes et cetera, et cetera."

"Typical Nigerian!" Tsola laughed. "Yes we all want to "ball", as you say, but given that no matter how much you earn, your resources are limited, if I asked you to narrow down what you want to three things this year, what would they be?"

"I honestly don't know," Zuri said. "I've never really thought about it. I guess the goal has just always been work hard, get promoted, earn more money, and the rest will work itself out."

"And therein lies the problem," Tsola said. "In fact, the money problems you are having now are just symptoms of an overarching problem. The real issue is you haven't articulated what you want the money you earn to do for you. So you let your resources be dragged in several directions that are not necessarily yours. If you had specific goals and a financial plan, you probably wouldn't be in this situation. Let me guess—you are the type of person who, if you had one hundred thousand in your account and your friends ask you to go on a trip to Ghana tomorrow and you know you have bills to pay in three months and no savings, you would go. Even though haven't planned for it?"

Zuri laughed. "Yup, I would probably go because you only live once, right?"

Tsola laughed with her. "I'm not saying you shouldn't go on holiday with your friends, *oh*! I'm just pointing out that you are probably an impulsive spender, hence your debt. I'm saying you need to get clear on what your goals are so you can spend and earn intentionally. For example, what are your priorities this year, in terms of money? Once you are clear on those things it'll be much harder for you to spend on the things that aren't as important to you.

"One of my goals this year is to finish building my house in Banana Island. So because of that, I've had to sacrifice a lot of things. Zuma gives board members an allowance for a new car every year, so typically I get a new one, but for the past two years I haven't. I've also had to give up going on our annual boys' trip to Marbella because it's usually a huge blow out where we spend a lot of money on yachts and champagne."

He laughed as Zuri rolled her eyes. "It's a lot of fun and a great way to let off steam because we all work so hard but this year, I have to skip it because I understand that it's a temporary sacrifice to make in the now, so I can achieve my long-term goal of building a house. Cut back on spending, save and invest more aggressively. Building materials have become more expensive but I'm certain it will be finished by first quarter next year."

"That's nice," Zuri said.

"So my point is, yes, it sucks that you are in debt but you earn enough that you can come out of it if you are disciplined and willing to make the spending sacrifices in the short-term so you can wipe out the debt. Also, are you maximising your earning potential? Are there other ways you could be putting your skill set to use so you could earn more money?"

"Hmmm. I don't know. I haven't really thought about it."

"Well, think about it. In fact, I have a small assignment for you," Tsola said.
"Will you do it?"
"*Ah ah*, are you now my teacher?" Zuri laughed. She saw the sober look on his face. She nodded.

"Okay, this is an exercise I did years ago in business school but it changed my life," Tsola said. "Do you have something to write with?"

Zuri pulled out the notebook and pen she always carried in her handbag and listened intently as Tsola began to dictate his instructions.

"When you get home tonight, write down what your perfect day would look like," he started.

"Huh? My perfect day! Ha! So you want me to start writing fairy tales now. I thought you were going to share some serious insight and drop something profound."

Tsola laughed. "Profound doesn't always have to be complex and you'll be surprised how difficult this actually is. Describe what your perfect day would look like in an ideal world. When you wake up in the morning what would you do? Where would you wake up? House or flat? What would you do? Pray? Meditate or exercise? All three? In what order? What do you do for work in your ideal life? What kind of car do you drive? What kind of holidays do you look forward to? Just describe the life you want!"

"This actually sounds fun. But then what?"

"Then, read it again, extract what three goals can you possibly achieve this year, and write down the things that would help you achieve them within a set timeframe. For example, maybe you want to be debt free? Let's imagine your debt is ten million naira. What actions would you have to take to smash that goal in three months?"

"Ten million, *ke*?" Zuri laughed. "*Abeg* o, my debt is nowhere that high."

"That's not the point—I'm just giving you an example. Your goal has to be specific, it has to have a timeline and you have to be clear on the actions you need to take to get there, whether the debt is one million or ten million. It could even be something like you want to go on holiday in the summer—how much would it cost? How long would it take to put the money aside? And what steps would you have to take to achieve these goals?" Tsola asked, reaching over to tuck a tendril of her hair behind her ear.

Hmm. Is he hitting on me? "I guess I really haven't given it that much thought. In terms of goals and everything," Zuri said.

"You can start with three goals for the year," Tsola said. "However, I usually set three goals per quarter for myself and three goals per quarter for my business. But you should start with three and get clear on what you want and then build from there. Break it down into manageable steps and then it won't seem so difficult."

"It makes a lot of sense when you put it that way," Zuri said, smiling.

As they landed in Benin, Zuri listened to Tsola talk about his work ambitions and dreams. She had never met anyone quite so sure of himself, but his ambition was actually contagious. She was inspired by his drive and commitment to doing whatever it took, to get what he wanted. It was as though he didn't understand the concept of failure or fear.

As they parted ways at the airport, she knew she was smitten. It was funny how you could talk to someone for months and never really have any deep conversations with them, but then you could meet someone, know them for barely a day and bare your soul to them. *I'm such a* saddo. *Wait. He didn't ask for my number. I thought we were connecting! Maybe it was one-sided.* She laughed at herself. She was already overthinking it. Tsola never said he was interested in her—he flirted a little bit and gave her some great advice but that was it. Why couldn't it just be that?

She had read a book years ago—'He's Just Not That into You', and it was enlightening. The book was derivative of the 'Sex and the City' series, and explored the idea that women spent too much of their time attempting to decipher the hidden meaning in things men *didn't* do or *didn't* say. Meanwhile, guys were supposedly quite simple: If they liked you, they asked you out. If they wanted to date you, they were pretty clear about it. Tsola seemed like a pretty straightforward guy. Maybe she wasn't his type? Maybe he just wasn't that into her? She laughed at herself for over-analysing the situation. He had probably already forgotten all about her.

> **SMART MONEY LESSON:
> ARTICULATE THE VISION
> YOU WANT FOR YOUR LIFE**
>
> The most successful people are the ones who are able to articulate what they want for their lives. Success is deeply rooted in having a solid plan that is tailored to what you want.

EXERCISE: ENVISION YOUR FUTURE

1. *Write down your vision statement. (What do you want your legacy to be?)*
2. *What are your short-term goals? What ten things do you need to do to achieve them?*
3. *What are your long-term goals? What ten things do you need to do to achieve them?*

CHAPTER 7:
THE SPENDING PLAN

"Have you finished eating?" Zuri's mother asked as she walked past the living room and beckoned to Osasu, the young girl who helped to look after Aunty Uwa's house, to take the dishes to the kitchen.

"Yes, Mummy. Thank you," Zuri replied with a satisfied smile. Her mother knew her well, one of the first things she had to eat when she got to town was *ogualigho*, a popular dish from a local *mama put* on Oba Market Road, near Siluko Junction in Benin City. It was basically perfumed rice with stew, but everything from its spicy aroma to its unique flavour put it above any other version of rice and stew as far as Zuri was concerned. It was a legendary *Bini* delicacy.

As Zuri lay sprawled on the sofa drifting in and out of her food coma, she heard footsteps approaching. Aunty Uwa was still away on a trip so it sounded like her mother had guests. She prayed they would go into the other room or stay in the kitchen but she knew that was just wishful thinking. Despite the fact that her mother knew she would prefer to be left alone with her thoughts, she wouldn't be able to resist showing off her 'daughter from Lagos' to whoever the visitor was. As the voices got closer, Zuri opened one eye to get a glimpse of who had come to visit.

Oh no. It is Aunty Grace, mum's friend from her days selling fabric in New Benin market. She can talk for hours.

"Zuri won't you get up and greet Aunty Grace," Her mother said, giving her a you-better-respect-your-elders look.

"Good Afternoon Aunty, it's been a while. How are... your kids?" Zuri said, struggling to remember their names.

"They are doing very well, *oh*. Peter lives in Germany now with his wife and two children, and Abigail is happily married with two children and another one on the way. I will soon have five grandchildren!

"Abigail lives in Lagos you know? You should get in touch with her maybe she can introduce you to someone; her husband has many eligible friends that are ready to get married. Have you found someone to marry now?"

"Not yet, ma," Zuri said with a forced smile. This was one thing she didn't miss about being in Benin. She would be dodging marriage questions all weekend.

Sensing Zuri's growing discomfort, her mother began to cough, her patented move to shut down any and all questionable conversation. "Zuri, please go to the kitchen and get me some water to drink. Grace, what would you like to drink?"

"Hmm my sister, that is it *oh, na so we see am*. These customs people just want to put someone out of business." Zuri heard as she walked back into the living room with refreshments.

"Can't that your agent handle it? I thought he was well connected at the ports?" Zuri's mum said.

"You mean Christopher? All the rules at the ports have changed!

Since they did the restructuring, they have sacked all the *ogas* that he knows there. So he is useless to me right now. I'm using one young guy but the money he's charging me to clear the goods is more than I bargained for."

Zuri pretended not eavesdrop. PHCN had taken light and so she made a big show of drifting round the room, drawing the curtains and opening up the windows so that the cool breeze could rescue them from the beginnings of the oppressive heat.

She could already tell where this conversation was going; she had witnessed this same exchange countless times. Today it was Aunty Grace, other times it was relatives or supposedly close friends, but regardless of who it was the *modus operandi* was the same. They would start by regaling Zuri's mother with a tale of misfortune. Although the stories varied, from problems with paying children's school fees abroad, medical bills or a sudden calamity that had befallen their business, the motive was always the same; she was their only hope and they needed her to lend them money. In Zuri's experience, these were loans that were never repaid.

In true form, Aunty Grace quickly got to the point of why she had paid them a visit in the first place.

"Mama Osahon, I know times are hard for everybody but I was hoping you would lend me some money to clear these goods, I already have customers that are willing to buy as soon as the fabric arrives. I will pay you back as soon as I sell."

As Aunty Grace started to sniffle, it became more difficult for Zuri to pretend that she wasn't listening to their conversation.

"Zuri, go and help Osasu in the kitchen with the *ogbono*, tell her we will have it with pounded yam for dinner," Zuri's mum commanded as she consoled Aunty Grace.

Zuri knew this was only a ploy to get her out of the room, so she wouldn't be there to witness her mother offer Aunty Grace money that she did not have. As she walked to the kitchen she couldn't help but wonder why her mother always did this. She had the habit of taking on everybody's problems at the expense of her own. She had done this since they were young, but it became disruptive after their father died and the family had to rely on one income instead of two.

Zuri's mother was very industrious, even though her husband made decent money as a civil servant. Her income from buying and selling everything from fabric to gold jewellery did a lot to supplement the family's income. However, as she grew older, Zuri realised with displeasure that she really didn't have any assets despite the fact that she had spent the better part of her life working really hard. In fact, Zuri didn't know many women from that generation that worked harder than her mother, but because over time she became everybody's 'big aunty', their go to person for handouts, she never had anything left to save or invest. Besides the house her father left, her mother had no other assets. She got a small stipend from her late husband's pension which was supplemented by the money Zuri's brothers sent from time to time but for the most part she was struggling in retirement and it was hard to watch.

Zuri watched from the kitchen window as her mother escorted Aunty Grace to her car. She could tell from their exchange that her mother had agreed to give the woman money.

"Why are you doing your face like that? You've come, *oh! Vbokhin?*" Her mother asked.

"Mummy you are asking me what? You know 'what' already? You have given that woman the money Osahon sent you to help repair the house?" Zuri admonished, even though she knew she wasn't going to get a direct answer.

"Did I tell you that? Please keep quiet, you think you know everything. Besides it's just a loan, I didn't *dash* her. She will pay me back." They both knew that this was a lie.

"Here we go again," Zuri said as she rolled her eyes. "Mummy we both know she is not going to pay you back'. Has she paid you back the last money she "borrowed" from you for her daughter's wedding?"

"My friend, *mind ya business*. It's good to help people when they are in need. It can happen to anybody. Besides that's why God is always blessing me and looks after my children for me."

"Okay mummy, let me ask you something. It's good to help people in need, right? But this woman heard your house almost burned down but she couldn't even be bothered to ask about you. Or how you were going to fix your house. What kind of person does that?" Zuri fumed.

Her mother walked out of the room.

Zuri couldn't but help but feel angry. Angry with her mother because she felt she should know better; Aunty Grace was never going to pay her back. Angry at herself because she knew if she didn't change her money habits this could be her life when she turned sixty too—albeit for different reasons.

* * *

"Hey girl, are you back in Lagos?"

Lara had called as soon as she touched down. "Yes love! How are you?" Zuri replied.

"I'm fine, *oh*, I just got off work. Let's hang out now? I'm in VI come and meet me at RSVP."

"With which money? How many times will I tell you my pockets are empty?"

"Okay, madam. Just come, I'll pay. Today was stressful. Need to let some steam off before I go home to face my mama's *wahala*."

"I'll see you in 20 minutes, if traffic doesn't kill us here."

* * *

Zuri spotted Lara as soon as she walked in, waving to get her attention. She was sitting at a table by the window in the back of the room. As Zuri walked towards Lara's table, she recognised a familiar face.

Tsola.

He was having dinner with three others and Zuri hesitated unsure if she should interrupt their conversation or avoid their table all together. As she struggled to make a decision, his eyes caught hers. He was smiling, so she decided to walk over to say hello.

"Hi! How are you?" he asked, as he stood up and kissed her on both cheeks and introduced her to the rest of his party. "What brings you here?"

She gestured in Lara's direction. "Lunch with a friend."

They chatted for a few more minutes.

"Ok let me let you get to it. We should catch up soon." He said with a smile.

"Good seeing you again." *Those smiles are just causing all sorts of confusion in my life.*

"Who was that?" Lara asked slyly.

"Oh, him? Just a guy I met at work," Zuri said trying to sound casual.

"Just a guy, *ke!* You were flirting like no tomorrow."

"You are not serious."

"Are you crushing on him? Does he work in your office? Is he toasting you? Spill!"

"Yes. No. I don't know." She hoped it would stop Lara from continuing her inquisition.

Lara crossed her arms and waited.

"Alright, alright! He was on my flight to Benin and we had a really great conversation. Actually, he was surprisingly easy to talk to, and we connected about some really deep stuff but then he didn't ask me for my number or try to contact me That was a week ago, so I figured he was just being polite, *oh jare*.

"Anyway he gave me some really good advice about money," Zuri rushed out, then continued to relay the whole saga behind their chance meeting.

"Wait, let me get this straight? You told a cute guy, you just met that you are broke? And now you are wondering why he didn't ask for your number?"

"Please, it's not a big deal! It just sort of came out. I wasn't thinking besides he didn't seem like he was judging me. Or was he?" Zuri said.

"Let me be honest. I'm your friend and I love you but I judged you small, *sha*, when you told me," Lara confessed.

That hurt. "Seriously?" Zuri replied.

"I said small. Calm down and let me explain. It's not that I'm best when it comes to saving or investing for that matter, but you have to be honest with yourself. We are grown women and this money stuff is important. Do you know how many people would kill for your salary? With what you earn you have no business saying you have no money. It is irresponsible. I am your friend so it is my responsibility to tell you the truth."

"I know, I know. I let it get out of hand," Zuri said.

"You don't have any excuse. You don't even have any real responsibilities. I look after my mother, pay school fees for my brothers and sisters, and still put money aside to save towards the future. Admittedly, not as much as I would like but at least it's something," Lara said.

"I'm really trying now, *sha*, but I can't lie, it is hard trying to pinch pennies and cut out a lot of things. I feel deprived. Actually let me be honest, since I paid off my debt it hasn't been easy to stick to the budget. In fact, Zazaii had a sale last weekend and I went a little overboard with my spending. I felt so ashamed the next day," Zuri said.

"That's the problem," Lara said consolingly. "You are going about it the wrong way. A budget is like a diet; if you start with an extreme diet and starve yourself, eventually you will binge and put on all the weight you lost in the first place. It has to be a lifestyle change; all this "Excel spreadsheet" you are trying to follow will *koba* you. Let me share something I learned a long time ago. Just keep it simple!"

"How?" Zuri felt more than a little frustrated. "There is nothing simple about saving."

"That's where you are wrong. You already know how much you need to survive with your spreadsheet. I divide my money into three different accounts—one for bills, another for long-term savings and an account for when spoiling myself with a new bag or trip. As soon as my salary is paid, I transfer the money to each account accordingly. To be honest it's become a habit, I don't think about it anymore. It just makes things easier," Lara said.

"Hmmm, that might actually work for me. It's funny how we've never talked about saving or investing. If we had this conversation a year ago, I probably would not have gotten into trouble in the first place."

Lara looked up to see a familiar face walking towards their table.

"Isn't that Tami?" Lara said.

"Oh, I forgot to mention that she was joining us," Zuri replied. "She called right after you did, and when I told her we were having dinner here she invited herself. You know she's obsessed with the cocktails here."

"Who isn't?" Lara laughed.

"Hey ladies! *Mwah*," Tami threw kisses at both her friends and settled into a chair.

Zuri took in Tami's outfit. It was a pink fitted dress with a white collar and what looked like this season's Céline Box Bag. "This dress is nice, *oh*, where is it from?"

"It's a TNL dress, I got it from Zazaii. I love that place, they have so many affordable Nigerian brands."

"Like who, *abeg*? I just spent a fortune there on their sale and it wasn't very affordable."

"See this one," Lara laughed. "It's because your eye will never see the ones that affordable, didn't you find any Lady Biba or Adey Soile dresses there? All reasonably priced with great value."

"Leave me, *jo*," Zuri said.

Lara laughed. "Meanwhile Tami, when did you get this Céline bag? It's new, *abi*? Please have you guys discovered a new bag connect? Hook us up, *na*! because this thing is not cheap and every fashion girl on Instagram seems to have it. I had lunch with Adesuwa last weekend and she just got the Watersnake version and she claimed it was a gift from Soji but I suspect it was retail therapy from her pocket to make herself feel better because of her "Soji stress". *Who be fool*? we all know that Soji ain't got it like that, I don't get why she bothers lying."

Tami and Zuri both burst out laughing.

"*Mehn, I tire oh*. We all know she is the breadwinner; why does she bother making up all these stories?" Zuri said. "Don't we see this everywhere? Most female breadwinners don't own up to the fact that they are the ones who are looking after their families. Even when they clearly earn more than their husbands, they keep up this charade that it's their husband looking after them. There's this woman in my office, she bought herself a car last month and then started telling everybody that her husband bought it for her. Like why though? What's the point?"

"If you ask Adesuwa, she'll say it is wisdom," Tami replied. "And, if you talk too much she'll say, 'you don't understand because you are not married', but personally I don't subscribe to that kind of arrangement. My own bag is a gift from that my new toaster, Uchenna. I saw it on Instagram and DMed him the picture to say that this was my new obsession. He brought it back from his last trip to London. This one has potential."

"You are not serious!" Lara laughed.

"*Ha*! I'm very serious. This is the type of husband I'm looking for," Tami said matter-of-factly. The type that can offer me financial security not these boy-men that will be expecting you to work so they can feed off you. I'm not about that life, *abeg*. When I become someone's wife I shouldn't have to work because I need to, I fully expect to work only because I want to have something to do."

Lara shook her head. "How are we friends? I'm honestly confused because I don't understand how you guys think about money. This one is broke." She pointed to Zuri. "Adesuwa is working hard only to allow her useless husband to mooch off her and spend her money chasing girls up and down Lagos."

Lara raised her eyebrows in Tami's direction. "You, you are waiting for a rich husband to provide financial security, *abi*? Listen, society and culture sells young African girls the lie that marriage is the financial security they should aspire to. Please, open your eyes! You have to learn to get yours. There are many women with rich husbands and no independence, either because their husbands are stingy or too controlling. Besides, what happens if he leaves you or dies? What then? You'll end being of those women who allowed themselves to be lulled into a false sense of security, then something happens to their marriage or husband dies and they wake up at forty years old not having a clue how to earn."

"Story." Tami laughed. "So now you want to marry a poor man, *abi*?"

Lara hissed. "See, you are missing the point! I'm not saying I don't want a rich husband. I have my own goals and dreams and I'd like to be able to bring value to a marriage and not depend solely on a man for my bread and butter."

"Tami, be there talking nonsense. Lara is teaching me how to budget and you should probably bring out your pen and paper and come and learn, too. I was just saying to Lara that we never have conversations about money unless it involves spending on food, fashion and flying."

They all laughed.

"But seriously guys, we need to start having more conversations about our goals and dreams and the money that will help to fund them," Lara said.

SMART MONEY LESSON:
DEVELOP A SUSTAINABLE BUDGET

One of the biggest issues people complain about when it comes to their money is not knowing how to save or budget. People associate the word "budget" with scarcity or a reduction in station of life. Therefore, "budget" is a word they come to resent. The reality is, a budget is something that tells you how to allocate your resources and it should reflect what you value. So if I looked at your bank statement, would it reflect that you are spending on the things you love or would it be a reflection of the fact that you don't spend intentionally and allow your money to be pulled in different directions?

The reason most people live paycheque to paycheque is because they don't have a full understanding of what their income can support. Money in the bank is equal to spending. It doesn't matter whether you earn ten thousand or ten million naira a month, your resources are limited and consumption tends to rise with income, so it's important to have a spending plan that takes that into consideration.

So here is the trick for guilt-free spending: the smart money budget! I know the idea of a budget makes most people nervous, but it shouldn't, especially if it's easy and reflects the things you love. The smart money budget is a way of allocating your resources.

First, divide your income into three parts:
- Long-term financial goals
- Short-term financial goals
- Living expenses

Long-term financial goals (LFG): At a minimum of twenty percent of your income, it represents a proportion set aside towards improving your net worth, i.e. buying assets that will provide you with an income. Good examples are towards purchases like land, property or a stock portfolio.

Short-term financial goals (SFG): The proportion of your income set aside for treats— a Chanel bag, an iPhone, or a luxury holiday; whatever tickles your fancy.

Living expenses: Your monthly contribution to your rent, health insurance, cable/satellite television, petrol, service charge etc.

Here are two examples of how differing incomes might look distributing a salary.

Lara:
Monthly income= ₦3,000,000
LFG (20%) = ₦600,000
SFG (10%) = ₦300,000
Living expenses (70%) = ₦2,100,000

Zuri
Monthly income= ₦600, 000
LFG (20%) = ₦120,000
SFG (10%) = ₦60,000
Living expenses (70%) = ₦420,000

EXERCISE: ORGANISE YOUR MONEY

Create buckets for different goals

1. An account for emergencies because you never know when your car is going to break down or when you have to send money to the village.
2. A 'turn up' account, because we work hard so we can play hard. Otherwise you'll be setting yourself up for overspending, which will jeopardise your financial freedom in the long run. (This could be for shopping, traveling, anything that makes you happy). Planning for it means you spend mindfully and within a budget, instead of impulsively.
3. An account for rent because it's easy to procrastinate and wait three or four months before the 'gbese' is due and then start panicking and borrowing. It's always better to have an account dedicated to this that you put aside systematically each month (this works for school fees as well).
4. An investment account because there's no point in working hard, year after year, earning three million naira a year, spending it all and then your net worth is one hundred and fifty thousand. It's best to systematically put aside a proportion of your salary toward building assets that will earn you an income.
5. An account for bills because Nigeria is expensive— this covers food, domestic staff's salaries, transport costs etc.

CHAPTER 8:
THE POWER OF NETWORKING

As the Uber car drove up to the entrance of Eko Hotel & Suites, Zuri was dreading the day ahead of her. It was the first day of WIMBIZ, a two-day conference filled with speeches, panel discussions, and breakout sessions. Determined not to suffer alone, she had convinced Adesuwa, Tami, and Lara to come and alleviate her boredom. Ladun wouldn't be coming because she was elbows-deep in preparation for her father-in-law's funeral.

Tami got one of her numerous 'toasters' to pay for her ticket, while Adesuwa's and Lara's companies had paid for their attendance. Lara's employers were keen on development apparently major sponsors for the event every year because they were passionate about developing the women on their staff, so they got a few complementary tickets for some staff each year. Adeswua's employer contributed to the event by bulk purchasing tickets for their female staff around the country, which was a substantial investment as there were over fifty of them.

"I'm always so impressed by how well-organised the WIMBIZ conferences are," Lara said as she flipped through the program.

"Really? How so? What makes it different from other conferences?" Zuri asked. "I guess I don't have anything to compare it to. I don't do all these Nigerian women events. I'm only here because Mr Tunde forced me and I'm still trying not to get fired."

Lara smiled. "I think you might find yourself pleasantly surprised. You might even learn something! Let's start with the fact that the registration process is so smooth, there are no queues because they text everyone codes beforehand, no one is complaining about not getting registration packs because there's more than enough. Plus, I think these Ankara laptop bags they've given everyone to put their WIMBIZ kit in are so pretty. It's the kind of thing you'll use over and over again."

Adesuwa nodded. "I completely agree with Lara. This has been a breeze compared to some of the Nigerian conferences I've been forced to attend. Two weeks ago I went to a conference that was so disorganised, I had to leave! After being in the registration queue for three hours—there was no sign of getting into the main hall. It was a rowdy mess. On the whole conferences are getting better, but, *mehn*, some of them are unforgivably bad."

"Apart from their organisational skills what else?" Zuri said, still sceptical.

"What do you mean, 'what else'?" Adesuwa said.

"I mean, let's be real ladies, in the words of Olamide, 'who WIMBIZ *epp*?'," Zuri laughed. "Do the young women who attend these conferences actually benefit from any opportunities or is it just story time? People have serious problems, *oh*! If Richmond Developments wasn't paying for me to be here I doubt I would be in a position to pay that much money to come and listen to motivational speeches and leave without the tools to actually make more money."

Adesuwa laughed. "I've heard that before but the truth is, I know many women who have benefited greatly from attending this conference. Last year I sat next to a girl I knew from university, she had just moved back to Nigeria and was looking for a job. During one of the panels she asked the country manager of a technology firm a question about an aspect of their business that was not being executed in Nigeria. The country manager asked to speak to her after the panel. Long story short, she landed a new job."

"Exactly! WIMBIZ is what you make of it," Lara said. "If you come here with a negative mind-set, looking for everything that's not perfect. You'll find exactly that. I know lots of women including myself who have made significant connections here that have led to fruitful business opportunities. Zuri, keep an open mind."

Zuri laughed. "Okay, I have heard! After all this hype, I just hope it's as good as you say."

"Please let's go inside and get our seats because they don't play with time," Lara said. "Has anyone called Tami? Why is she always late? They don't let you save seats here. Please can someone text her? If she doesn't make it on time, she probably won't be sitting with us. She'll have to sit in the back."

"You know Tami, doesn't wake up early," Zuri laughed. "She sent her assistant to register for her. She promised to be here before ten a.m. I'll try to save her a seat. Let's go inside."

"Ah it's true, *oh*, I didn't notice before but you look hot, especially for a workday," Adesuwa said. "This is a women's event *oh*, no men here!" She laughed. "Makeup on point and your outfit screams power woman."

"Thanks guys. I just wanted to look nice today. Is it a crime?" Zuri laughed. As they walked past the sliding doors, Zuri caught a glimpse of her reflection. The electric blue Obsidian suit was always a good idea, and today she'd paired the trouser suit with a crisp white button up shirt. She was channelling Betty Irabor, the publisher of *Genevieve* magazine, Nigeria's answer to *Glamour*. Now, that was a woman with style and she had that power woman look down to perfection, especially when she wore a suit. She had seen her in a navy blue silk Deola Sagoe suit once, and she'd looked beyond fantastic.

She didn't tell the girls but she had taken special care with her appearance this morning mostly because Mr Tunde had called her earlier to say they had a meeting with Zuma Capital at 6:00 p.m., so she had to come back into the office after the conference. This was hopefully the last in a series of meetings they had been having with the partners from Zuma over the last six weeks. Tsola had been in a few of them and they had chatted like friends, but he had been mostly business-like and still hadn't asked for her number.

Zuri felt silly that she was still thinking about him in this way. The girls had started mocking her because they claimed that in the last couple of weeks, she'd found new ways to slide his name into the conversation.

She didn't know what it was about him, but she couldn't get him out of her head. She had never met anyone like him. It was weird because the vibe he gave off was 'I like you' and 'I love talking to you' but he never made a move. Which made her think maybe he had a girlfriend or a wife because this was Nigeria, it was completely normal for a married man to be flirting with you and 'forget' to mention he had a wife at home but she had done some digging and no one ever saw him publicly with a wife or girlfriend.

Zuri shook herself out of her Tsola daze as proceedings began. *Here we go.*

* * *

By the end of the third panel discussion, Zuri was a bona fide convert. There were over a thousand women in the hall and the energy was electric. It was a multi-generational platform, where women who were at the top of their game could interact with young women who were just starting out and share their experiences and learnings on their journey to success. It was truly invigorating. She was excited about the possibilities but at the same time she had this sense of, *what have I been doing with my life?* These women were not only making a killing financially, they were making a huge positive impact and changing lives.

As she washed her hands and prepared to leave the restroom, she noticed a woman struggling with her skirt zipper.

"Should I help you with that?" Zuri asked.

"Yes please, it's always a nightmare trying to get this zip back up," she replied. Zuri deftly dealt with the unruly zipper. "Thank you! I'm Ijeoma but you can call me '*Nwanyi Akamu*' or '*Iya Ologi*'."

Zuri laughed, slightly confused. *Akamu* or *ogi* as it was called in Igbo or Yoruba languages referred to a local breakfast pap, which was fermented cereal pudding, made out of maize or millet. The women who were referred to as '*Nwanyi Akamu*' or '*Iya Ologi*' were usually known for selling the dish at the side of the road, miles apart from the well-dressed, well-spoken woman with whom Zuri was conversing.

Colour me intrigued, she thought. "You sell *ogi*?" Zuri asked.

"Yes, I do," Ijeoma replied with a knowing smile. "Updated and with a modern twist! They come in yoghurt-like packaging and in different flavours like strawberry and banana."

Still deep in conversation as they walked into the lunchroom together, Zuri listened to her talk passionately about her business, how it had started in her kitchen but now had its own factory and had grown to distributing to over thirty outlets across Nigeria.

Ijeoma worked the lunchroom, stopping to greet and sometimes introduce herself to some of the women in the room, then proceed to explain to Zuri who they were—Tara Fela-Durotoye, owner of House of Tara, the first home-grown makeup brand and makeup training school; Bolanle Austen-Peters, owner of Terra Kulture and successful playwright.

"Have you signed up for speed mentoring?" Ijeoma asked as they headed out the dining area preparing to part ways.

"No, I haven't. What's that about?" Zuri asked.

"It's a twenty-minute session where they pair mentees with potential mentors and they have a quick discussion about their goals, career progression and any obstacles they might be facing at work or in their business," Ijeoma explained. "It's really phenomenal."

"I could definitely use a mentor! I'll go and sign up after lunch," Zuri replied. WIMBIZ was definitely looking more and more worth it.

Ijeoma had to head to her next session and so asked she Zuri for her business card. As they exchanged details, Ijeoma explained further. "Just remember, each mentor is probably going to meet at least twenty prospective mentees, so do your best to be memorable and lead with the highlights, the things that make you memorable. You want to engage them in the first few minutes. In short? Don't be boring!" Ijeoma laughed as she waved goodbye.

As Zuri scoured the hall for her friends, she couldn't help but think about how fantastic the networking opportunities at the conference were—every woman who was doing anything substantial in Nigeria was here. It didn't even matter the industry—oil and gas, finance, interior design, event planning, and even women from the public sector—there were connections to be made. Zuri couldn't believe that she'd been so resistant to coming.

"Lara, you were so right, this is beyond everything I expected!" Zuri said excitedly during a break. "I'm truly inspired. I've met so many interesting people, and everyone's been so supportive and encouraging. What about you guys? Have you met anyone interesting?"

"Well, I m—" Lara started.

Tami rushed up and interrupted, "Oh my gosh! I just met my

Instagram crush, that Nnenna Okoye woman that owns Youtopia Beauty. Her skin is so fresh. She is the best ambassador for her brand. Like, you don't understand! Since I discovered Youtopia I don't have to beg people coming from "the abroad" to buy my products. She basically curates best products from around the world and delivers them right to your doorstep."

"*Awon* Instagram "celebs"," Lara scoffed.

Tami said, "See you. One thing I've learnt at this conference is that some of us are using Instagram to play while others are using it to build platforms and audiences in order to *sell dia market*. You, Lara, that swears by Dooney's Kitchen recipes, how did you discover them? Or Adesuwa, didn't you put Junior on a routine based on tips you found on parenting from Maky's Corner? I'm even going to start following She Leads Africa on Instagram because of their focus on women and business. People are doing things on social media that are really changing how people connect.

"I just had a conversation with a girl and she said '*Dey dere*... Instagram is life', and the people who don't get that are just like the people in the nineties who said that the internet was the big bad wolf and would destroy us. I had to laugh at that one, but maybe she has a point, you know. Social media is the new way we interact. Not just with our friends but it's how we showcase our products, acquire customers and grow our businesses."

"I hear you! But before you interrupted me, I was about to tell Zuri that I met Nimi Akinkugbe. She's basically a personal finance rock star! She used to be the head of wealth management at Stanbic IBTC for ages, then left to join Barclays Wealth, now she's the CEO of

Bestman Games, the company that brought Monopoly to Nigeria. She is so well-spoken and so proper. I'm obsessed! Anyway, she suggested we go to the Money Makeover breakout session that's about to start," Lara said.

"You guys go ahead, let me just dash to the House of Tara booth to freshen up my makeup and look at what they have for sale," Tami tossed over her shoulder as she hurried off.

Zuri and Lara walked briskly to their session, and just managed to catch it as a statuesque woman started speaking. "Hello ladies," she was saying. "My name is Omosede and I am passionate about personal and business finance. To get started, I'd like us all to introduce ourselves, say what we do for a living, share what we are deeply passionate about and share the main reason we chose to attend this breakout session."

After everyone had finished their introductions, Omosede addressed the whole room again.

"So we all want to be rich, right? Let's talk a little bit about the things we believe are stopping us from attaining wealth. Impulsive spending? Not enough money? Too many bills? Yup, those are all issues, I agree, but they are only the symptoms of the problem. The biggest issue most of us have with money is we don't understand how it works, so no matter how much we make, we can't seem to get to the place called financial freedom.

"In my experience men are more aggressive when it comes to building wealth. It might be cultural or a product of patriarchy, but men and women are raised to think about their money differently.

Most African men are taught early on that they are the providers, so they want to generate enough income that will protect their family's financial future. Therefore, men are more likely to want to be landlords and take on more risks like invest in the stock market, so they can grow their money faster.

"My theory is that most African women are great at saving but they tend to save to spend instead of saving build. I think it's because we are raised to be nurturers, so any extra income often translates to more money spent on improving the immediate—extras for the kids or money to make the house a home. She may even be contributing a significant amount to the household, to rent and school fees. They are great things to save towards but they also aren't assets, so once that money is paid, it's gone. We don't put as much weight on building assets that will provide us with an income in the future and protect our financial future because 'it is a man's job.'"
That made Zuri think.

It was a great session and Zuri loved that Omosede had taken the time to lay out a thorough 'game plan' that allowed for focus and direction without being too complicated. All the lessons she had learned from Tsola, her own mistakes and even Lara all seemed to come together in this room, in such a powerful way.

Omosede started to round up the session, with some hard hitting truths and words of hope. "We all have X amount of productive years to work and earn a living. If you can't find a way to save and invest toward assets that will provide you with an income when you have the ability to earn, what happens when you are sixty and you've spent all the income you've ever earned?

"We all hope we'll earn more money, make that huge transaction that will make us billionaires, but ultimately what is most important is our money mind set. The way we *think* about money. Ultimately, what makes us wealthy is not how much we earn but how we can systematically use a proportion of the income we earn to build assets that pay us over time."

When Omosede was finished speaking, the whole room erupted in enthusiastic applause. The message had truly connected, and Zuri could feel how each woman was, right then and there, resolving to change the way she thought about money.

Zuri really wanted to meet the speaker after the session. Omosede was inundated with people seeking her attention however, and with Zuri needing to rush in to the office for the signing with Zuma, she simply grabbed what information she could and headed to the lobby to catch her ride.

* * *

It was almost seven thirty in the evening when Zuri got to the office. She had gotten a text postponing the meeting and she was right on time. Her mentoring session had gone so well that Mrs Abafo-Williams, a partner in a law firm that specialised in corporate law, had asked her to look for her after all the sessions were done, so they could talk some more. There was no way Zuri would have missed her; she was wearing a fabulous Lanre Da Silva dress. She was one of the most beautiful, impeccably dressed women Zuri had ever met and was equally as intelligent. Zuri had only ever seen her on TV and read about her in magazines and newspapers. She was equally known for style and her ability to close some of the biggest financial transactions in recent years. She was just as well regarded as any man in her field and Zuri was in awe of her. The advice she had already passed on with regards to Zuri's work in real estate was invaluable. It gave Zuri a new perspective and a plan had already begun to form in her mind. They had arranged to meet for coffee in the coming weeks.

With the papers duly signed by both teams and the photography and interviews underway, signing had gone smoothly, and the Zuma team seemed pleased with the deal. Exhausted from her day at WIMBIZ and the signing, Zuri decided to sneak out early, ordering a cab to a rear entrance of the office in order to escape a little early, leaving the other still chatting.

"Hello," a masculine voice said. Zuri turned around to see that it was Tsola.

"Hi." She was trying not to give away that she was shy. "Is the meeting still on?"

"No," He said with a smile. "We finished about fifteen minutes ago. The others just left… I stayed behind to respond to some emails in the lobby before I jump into my car, then I spotted you here."

"Would you like to have a drink with me?" Tsola said. "To celebrate the fact that we've finally signed the agreement!" He quickly added.

"Hmmm," Zuri mused with a playful smile. "Isn't that a bit odd? Celebrating without the rest of the team?"

He smiled. "Okay, you got me! I'd like to take you out for a drink because I like you. I've had a bit of a crush on you since we met."

Zuri tried not to blush. "Really? You certainly didn't give that impression. After our intense conversation on the flight to Benin, you never even asked for my number, and all I got was a we-are-strictly-colleagues vibe from you."

Tsola smiled. "You know I had to. I don't like to mix business with pleasure, so it was important that the deal close first. Now Folake will be the lead on this transaction, so our interaction on a business level won't be an issue."

"Got it."

"How about that drink?"

"Sounds good."

"So tell me about this special conference."

As they walked to his car, she told him about her WIMBIZ experience, her initial scepticism, how it had her changed her world view, her incidental meeting with Ijeoma in the ladies' room and how the networking tips she got from her landed her a possible mentorship with Mrs Abafo-Williams.

He looked intrigued.

They ended up choosing Craft Gourmet for dinner and were settled in quickly in a discreet corner of the restaurant. They placed their order along with a couple of glasses of white wine.

"Have you managed to solve your money *wahala*?" Tsola asked.
Zuri smiled. "Sort of. I paid off all my debts, so my landlord has

finally stopped hounding me."

"That's good."

"But I'm still a little confused about the whole investing thing, and I met a super cool babe today, that seems to get it but by the time she was done talking, there were so many women around her I couldn't talk to her one on one."

"Really? Who was she?"

"Her name is Omosede Ighodalo. She works at Concord."

"Oh, Omo? I know her, we went to business school together. She's brilliant. I can set up a meeting with her for you if you want."

"Would you?"

"Sure. I'll call her this week and see what her schedule is like. In fact, I have a small gift I've been meaning to give you. Nothing fancy, but remember those goals we talked about? I think this might help."

"What is it?" Zuri asked as she unwrapped the box.

"A money journal. I saw it and thought of you. It will help you articulate your thoughts on what your goals are, track your spending and write down that vision statement."

Zuri had to smile. It was the sweetest thing that anyone had done for her in a while. "Thank you. This is really thoughtful of you."

The waiter appeared with their meals and they spent the evening talking about their childhoods, their dreams, their goals, and ambitions.

Tsola spent the evening disproving the generalisation that all kids that came from wealthy backgrounds were lazy. His parents had made a lot of money in agriculture, but it was important for him to hustle. The way he was passionate about his work and his dedication to it was very different from her ex Folabi, who had also come from money but was content to merely spend his parent's instead of earn his own.

The man was good looking, but more than that, she was starting to realise that good conversation was her kryptonite.

SMART MONEY LESSON: YOUR NETWORK IS YOUR NET WORTH

Having an extensive network allows you to maximise your potential. There are no level playing fields, but it can be argued that in Nigeria the field is a little more uneven. A person's ability to attract wealth is tightly linked to how well they are able to grow and leverage his or her network to take advantage of opportunities.

The operative word here is "leverage". Lots of people from wealthy backgrounds have parents who lunch with some of the country's most powerful men and women, but they are unable to leverage those connections—combined with their talent—and translate it to money. On the other hand, plenty of folks who came from less privileged backgrounds have been able to parlay their way into certain circles by virtue of the value they add.

Mentorship is an awesome way to build your network and accelerate your personal growth, but instead of having the 'Aunty, *epp* me' approach, it's better to try to build organic relationships. You want a mentor who is invested in your growth and genuinely wants you to succeed. This is more likely when you have built a relationship and they become genuine friends as opposed to a transactional relationship that feels obligatory.

Okay, I know conventional wisdom at networking events is

usually *'sell ya self, sell ya mark*et', but take a minute to think about the fact that a thousand other women are doing just that. So, *what* makes you different? I can't tell you how many conversations I overheard that started with, 'My name is XYZ, I'm into Brazilian hair' or 'I'm into fashion. The concept of my business *is blah, blah, blah'*. Let me tell you a secret. They'll smile, they'll nod, they'll even take your business card but girl, no one cares about your CV or business concept for that matter! You know why? It sounds rehearsed, and limits chances for genuine conversation.

Instead of talking about yourself, ask questions about the other person, find common points of interest and then work interesting titbits about yourself into the conversation.

Elevator pitches are important, but people are more likely to connect with you if you can sell them on your 'why' as opposed to what you do. For example, instead of saying, 'My name is Anire and I make smoothies—we have apple, strawberry and pineapple flavours', try saying, 'I used to be so depressed about my weight but last year I lost fifteen kilos with a smoothie-inclusive diet and decided to start a business that will help other women like me lose a ton of weight'. You are probably going to be more memorable this way.

The business or job opportunities you'll have access to will come from your ability to harness your network and learn how to convert that network into opportunities because the more people you are able to reach and influence, the more likely you are to attract new business, gain access to partnerships or raise funding for your business.

EXERCISE: GROW YOUR NETWORK

1. Evaluate your network. Who do you know? Who is in your circle of friends?
2. Promote, demote, add and subtract. You are the CEO of your life, you shouldn't be giving time to people or relationships that do not add value.
3. What professional organisations do you belong to?
4. How active are you in said organisations? It is one thing to be a member but another to be recognised as someone who adds value.
5. Articulate and perfect your non-elevator pitch with practice, practice, practice.

CHAPTER 9:
LIFE HAPPENS

The music playing in Tsola's Range Rover was loud and raw. Zuri couldn't make out who the rapper was but Tsola seemed so hype as he rapped along to the lyrics. He was definitely a fan. This was just one of the many things that intrigued her about him; buttoned-up finance *efiko* one minute, rapper of every lyric from Jay-Z's 'The Blueprint' album the next. His tastes were diverse too, bumping everyone from Fela and KWAM 1 to Drake and Young Jeezy. It had been a fun couple of months getting to know him. His likes, dislikes, his little quirks; she was starting to understand what made him tick.

"What exactly is this mess we are listening to?" Zuri teased as she gave him the side eye.

"You mean 'Uncle Akala, the flow *fada*'?" Tsola replied, looking amused. "It's Akala, a conscious rapper from London. His music is the truth!"

"That's what you say about all the music you listen to."

"No, seriously, this guy has amazing depth. You should google some of his talks about social injustice and structural racism," Tsola said earnestly.

Zuri smiled. Tsola was a man of deep passions, be it about his friendships, family, or even her. The way he introduced her to friends and family made her blush, describing her to them in a way that made her recall about the kind of woman she aspired to be. It was as though he only saw the best version of her and it inspired her to commit to becoming just that.

The ringing from her phone interrupted her thoughts. It was her mother.

She gestured at Tsola to turn down the volume as she picked up the phone. "It's my mother, you know she won't stop calling until I answer."

Tsola smiled and nodded knowingly.

"Hello mummy, how are things?" Zuri said

"Fine, *oh*, my daughter, we thank God," Zuri said. "They've almost finished all the work on the house, it's just the painting that remains then I can finally leave Aunty Uwa's house and move back home."

"I'm so happy to hear that, Mama."

She and her siblings had been contributing money in the last few months to help the repairs the parts of the house that got damaged in the fire. It had been tight but she was glad to be able to help her mum. It gave her a sense of fulfilment.

"How is Ladun coping? Today is the funeral, *abi*?" Zuri's mother queried. "My friend Iyabo was telling me that there's infighting in the family. Quarrel over money and all sorts since the baba died."

"Hmmm, mummy. She's doing as well as expected, given the circumstances. To be honest I'm still not exactly sure what the details are, all I know is that they are in some kind of financial trouble since Baba Ashoni died. I haven't heard anything about fighting so far, and Ladun just sounds scared. It's been difficult to talk to her because there has just been so much going on in their house."

"It must still be a shock. Death brings out the ugliness in people, especially where money is concerned. You must advise her to *shine her eye*," Zuri's mother warned. I remember when your father died. I saw a side to his family I had never seen before."

"I remember."

Even though she had been a teenager, the bitter memory of the way her father's brothers had come to the house right after his death to ransack his study for property documents lingered with Zuri.

"I was still in mourning when your uncles tried to throw us out of the house. They even accused me of killing their brother. If not for Aunty Uwa, I'm not sure what I would have done."

"Can you just imagine?" *All because of money*.

'Yes, *oh*, my daughter. They took everything they could lay their hands on. Aunty Uwa and her sisters kept saying I should have secured all the documents for the property your dad owned before they came, but my husband had just died. That was the last thing on my mind. I just wanted to mourn my husband in peace. Besides I didn't even know what to look for."

The whole situation had been insane. The uncles that she knew vaguely from holidays in the village had transformed into menacing men who had terrorised them all. Trauma aside, Zuri also recalled that Aunty Uwa and her sisters had fought her uncles with everything they had, helping her mum lay claim to her father's house and his pension. He hadn't left a will, so it had been difficult to reclaim his other property that was taken, plus, her mother had been too tired to fight.

"Mummy, I have to go. Tsola and I are on our way to the funeral reception now."

'Ah! Greet Tsola for me, *oh*," a very pleased voice practically sang back at Zuri. Her mum *loved* Tsola.

"Mummy sends her love," Zuri said as she rolled her eyes. She knew what was coming next. Ever since her mother got wind of her relationship with Tsola, the frequency of her phone calls had increased. She was calling *per second, per second*, waiting for news of marriage. They had been dating for barely two months and the woman was ready to start sending out wedding invitations.

"So do you think he's going to propose soon," Zuri's mother had asked with a seriousness that made Zuri want to simultaneously burst out laughing and scream with frustration.

"No mummy, It's too early, *now*. Anyways, I have to go I'm being rude," Zuri said, trying to put an end to the conversation.

"We will continue this later. I just want to know what his intentions are. Do you need to date for one hundred years before he knows he wants to marry you?"

Sigh. "Bye, mummy."

Zuri got off the phone and grinned at Tsola.

"What's too early?" Tsola asked

"Marriage." Zuri said, looking him dead in the eye.

"Huh?"

"She wanted to know if you were going to propose soon and I said it was too early," Zuri said with a boldness that she hoped would throw him off guard.

"How do you know I'm not ready to marry you now?" Tsola grinned.

"Whatever, *oga,* please face the road," Zuri said playfully. In her head she wondered if he was serious.

The hall was rowdy when they got there. There were over a thousand people in attendance and it was difficult to see where her friends were seated over the sea of multi-coloured *gele*—each hue representing yet another family faction. Between the blaring live music and the overly-animated, slightly inappropriate MC, to a non-Nigerian it would be difficult to tell that this was indeed a funeral. This was the Yoruba way, however; Baba was over eighty when he died, so it was a celebration of a man who had a full life instead of a period of mourning.

The immediate family would be having a very different experience, mourning not necessarily only because Baba had died, but also for the lifestyle they had lost.

***

This mess is straight out of a movie, Ladun thought. In the span of two short weeks, they had lost almost everything. Come to think of it, had they really ever owned it? It was more than obvious now that the lifestyle to which they had become accustomed had been completely borrowed. Neither Bode nor his siblings had been fully aware, although they all worked in the business. As the news of Baba's heart attack spread the banks had come running—and life as the Ashoni clan knew it came to a crashing halt.

The family business had been bleeding cash for some time, and all their homes had been mortgaged in futile attempts to save it. The banks had given the family notice: if the loans weren't repaid in thirty days, the homes would all be repossessed. This included Baba's house in Ikoyi as well as the homes of Bode and his two brothers. It was all a shock. It seemed the banks no longer believed in the Ashoni name, now that the patriarch was gone.

Still, Ladun was unsurprised they were having this big party for his funeral. They definitely couldn't afford it but this was Lagos; it was what was expected of the Ashoni's and they still had a name to protect.

Bode and his brothers weren't being realistic about the situation. In the last few weeks all they had been concerned with was planning a big shindig for the funeral. Bode tried to convince her that they had the financial situation under control but with each passing day, it got worse and worse. And to top it off, Baba had also taken on too much personal debt. Ladun's thoughts raced as she considered the ramifications. *My God. Where will we live? Can we still afford Brookings Primary for the children? Going on holiday this summer is completely out of the question, but the cancelled tickets will give us some much needed funds.*

Ladun had confided in the girls, and Lara had advised that she brush up her résumé to find a job, while Tami suggested she consider starting a business. Having spent almost ten years as a pampered, hardworking housewife, the nine-to-five world had passed her by. Bode had taken care of her every whim since they'd started dating, so she had nothing of her own

As she tried to beckon to the waiter to serve small chops to the table next to her, she felt a strong grip on her arm and turned around to see who it was. It was Tsola, Zuri's new boo.

"Oh, hello Tsola," Ladun said. "I was starting to wonder if you guys were here."

"They sent me to find you. We are on that table over there in the corner," Tsola gestured to where her friends all sat a few metres away.

***

Zuri watched as Ladun and Tsola approached the table. *Tsola is such a gentleman.* She couldn't make out what they were saying but she was sure he was comforting Ladun in some way. She and Tsola had slotted in to each other's lives over the last few weeks, attending almost every event together as though they were joined at the hip. She was happier than she had been in a long time.

Zuri looked at Ladun as she walked away after the quick chat, and she noticed that Ladun looked gaunt. Tragedy would do that to you. She wondered how she and her family were coping with both the death and the unwelcome surprise of their new circumstances. *Families need to have real conversations about money,* oh. *What is it? The only time that seems to happen is when a breadwinner dies and they leave their money situation in tangled mess... no will, accounts and property all over the place, debt nobody knows about. Look at what this* wahala *is doing to this family now. And you know Africans. If you ask, they will tell you 'are you planning to kill me?'.* Zuri smiled to herself.

Lara looked at Zuri. "What's so funny?"

Coming out of her reverie, she replied, "Sorry, I didn't realise I was being obvious. I was just thinking about wills."

"Wills? How are those funny?" Tsola asked.

"You know, no matter how many times we hear these stories about families going into financial ruin after the death of the patriarch, nothing ever changes. Rich, poor, or in between, *oh,* nobody writes a will. There's so much paranoia and superstition when it comes to discussing family finances and it doesn't make any sense."

Tsola shook his head and said, "You are even going too far. The funniest thing is when they put their brothers as next of kin on all their bank accounts instead of their wife or child. It's depressing. I mean, how exactly do they expect their families to survive? The thing is everybody always thinks their own brothers are different, but the fact is when money is involved, greed brings out the worst monsters in all of us."

"The worst thing is, it's not just our parents' generation, it's us too," Adesuwa chimed in. "Soji and I never talk about money without tension. At first it was normal because that's how I grew up as well, my parents never really discussed money with us or with each other. But now with everything that's going on, I realise it's something we should have discussed even before we got married. The last fight was so bad. I haven't seen him in two days."

Zuri and Lara exchanged concerned looks.

"What's going on with Soji now?" Lara asked.

"Hmmm," Adesuwa sighed heavily. "In the last couple of weeks he's been withdrawing unusually large amounts of money from our joint account and every time I try to ask, it turns into this huge fight. He'll say I have no respect and that I only have the guts to question him because his businesses are not doing well and I'm making more money. God knows, that is not my intention! I honestly don't care who makes more. I just worry because we have so much debt and our expenses keep rising. I've realised that Soji is more of an impulsive spender than me. I'd rather look at my pocket first before I spend but Soji's mentality is spend now and worry about it later."

"So you have no idea what he's spending it on? I hope he's not in trouble," Zuri said even more worried about this new revelation.

"If you don't mind me asking, does all the money you make go in the joint account Adesuwa?" Tsola asked cautiously. "You don't have to answer if you don't want to. The situation just sounds a bit worrying."

"It's fine. I'm not offended because, to be honest, I don't know what to do anymore. To answer your question, yes, all of my salary goes into that account. I don't even know what to think anymore. Sometimes, I think maybe he is in some kind of trouble and doesn't know how to tell me, which is why he's being so defensive.

"Other times, I think it's another woman. But he can't be that stupid. Soji knows how much debt we've taken on for his businesses and how much of a struggle it is to pay our bills every month. He would never spend that kind of money on another woman."

"Adesuwa! Adesuwa! Wake up! How can you allow this man to continue spending your hard earned money like this?" Lara burst out, frustrated at her friend's unwillingness to face the truth. "At the very least, you have the right to ask questions about what he's spending it on."

"Lara you don't understand because you are not married," Adesuwa said, defensive. "Soji's ego is very fragile right now because he hasn't had success with his last few ventures, and I just have to be patient and employ wisdom. At the end of the day, I don't want to break my home over money. For all I know maybe he's taking the money out to do another business that will turn out to be better for our family in the long run and he just doesn't want to talk about it. I just have to keep praying. This is just a rough patch. I just need to persevere."

Lara looked like she was about to explode again, but Zuri clasped her hand tightly underneath the table to hold her back. Clearly, Adesuwa was still in denial but there was nothing they were going to say to her that would change her mind.

Tsola pushed back gently. "I completely understand where you are coming from Adesuwa but can I suggest something? Open another account and start putting some of your salary in it. I don't think it's healthy for a couple with two different ideas about money to have a joint account for everything. Something that's worked for a lot of my married friends is having separate individual accounts, but having a joint account for expenses that have to do with the household and an agreed percentage that each party contributes from their earnings. It's just easier that way."

For a moment, Adesuwa's pride resisted the idea. Then she crumbled. "I wish I had done that from the start because it would be so much easier to implement. But now? I don't know," she said with despair.

* * *

It was almost 9:00 p.m. as Adesuwa drove home from the funeral. She still hadn't heard from Soji all day and till now, she still hadn't been able reach him. She had hoped that he would surprise her and show up to support Ladun and Bode at the funeral, but this wasn't the first time he'd let her down.

Her phone rang.

"Hello, Soji?"

"No ma, this *na* Friday."

The security guard. "Oh," she replied, disappointed. "Any problem?"

"Madam, diesel *go soon finish and oga no dey. I be wan remind you because e no go reach till tomorrow.*"

"Okay, thank you." She was tired of the incessant costs that seemed to constantly assault her.

As she drove around trying to find the nearest ATM, she wondered where exactly Soji was. She had called all his friends and they all feigned ignorance as usual. She wished there was someone he feared or at least respected. Someone she could call to talk some sense into him and encourage him to adjust his behaviour. Soji resented his father for leaving his mother to start another family and they had no meaningful relationship, so there was no point even bothering to go that route. His mother had clung to religion a little too tightly to help her through her trying times, and now wielded a twisted version like a club, beating Adesuwa over the head with it, and blaming her daughter-in-law for her son's failures.

She would ask Adesuwa about private matters that didn't concern her and insist that the Holy Spirit told her to ask. She would even use scriptures from the Bible to justify Soji's bad behaviour, and insist that Adesuwa not being Christian enough or brought up well enough was why Soji didn't stay at home. "*Ah! Shebi* it is you that wants my son to provide? He is out looking for money, so why are you complaining? Besides, you are a heathen and your marriage is not built on a strong foundation of Christ. That is why you are having all these problems," she would tell Adesuwa.
It took a while but Adesuwa began to realise that Soji's mum did not like her, and the little jabs which seemed innocent at first were designed to chip at her confidence. Sometimes Adesuwa was tempted to asked her mother-in-law a question that seemed

obvious to everyone but her—if Soji had been raised in such a devout Christian home, why was his behaviour so questionable? If she as his mother wasn't able to convert her son to Christ in the thirty-odd years she had raised him before Adesuwa came along, why was it all of a sudden Adesuwa's responsibility?

Despite these painful memories, she was considering calling her mother-in-law to ask if she had heard from Soji, then she remembered the other issues the woman had with her. More recently, her issues with Adesuwa had been two fold. First of all, Adesuwa was getting too proud because she was the breadwinner and, secondly she questioned why they didn't have a second child. The woman's constant snide commentary on both matters only fuelled Soji's resentment and further soured their marriage.

"Insufficient balance, *ke*?" Adesuwa said out loud, as the flashing warning on the screen of the ATM shocked her back to reality.

How can the balance on the account be insufficient, when I'm only trying to take out ten thousand? I just got paid. These banks and the stupid Interswitch. What is this nonsense, now? Let me check my balance.

Four naira, eighty-three kobo. She couldn't believe what her eyes were seeing. *How? This must be some kind of mistake.* Adesuwa thought in panic. She dialled frantically, calling Soji again and again. No answer.

NO. He can't have done that to me. To us.

She walked back to her car, tears streaming down her face as she wrestled with accepting the truth. *Has Soji taken all our money and abandoned me with his debt? What will I do?*

SMART MONEY LESSON: THE CONVERSATION ABOUT FAMILY FINANCES MUST BE HAD

In Africa, discussions of money and assets in a family in the context of what happens when the breadwinner dies are almost taboo, and as a result this leads to disputes within families when the inevitable happens. We need to have more conversations about estate planning and wills. In simple terms, how assets will be divided in case of death and who the beneficiaries are. Women need to start asking tough questions about life insurance, debt, deeds, brokerage accounts, trusts and in general where financial records are kept, who is on the next-of-kin form et cetera. In the event where the woman has no formal occupation and no income of her own, she is protected. It is better to be prepared beforehand than to wait for tragedy to occur before these discussions are had.

In addition, when couples are coming together money matters should be a well-considered part pre-marital counselling. A discussion about the expectations of each person's responsibility is critical. We all come from different backgrounds and carry our own money biases and habits, and we often assume a synergy with our significant. For example, Sade and Femi get married and live together for the first time. Sade comes from a home where her mother was a housewife and her father the provider, so even though she works for a living her notion is 'my money is my money, and Femi's money is our money'. If

Femi comes from a family where both parents contributed equally to the household and believes strongly that Sade should contribute to the household expenses, without a proper discussion, this can cause significant problems.

There is also the issue of understanding each other's money personalities; establishing who is the saver and who is the spender early on and to protect both parties. It is probably best to keep personal finances separate but have a joint account for household expenses with pre-agreed amounts that each person contributes.

EXERCISE: TAKE STOCK OF YOUR FAMILY FINANCE

1. What are your assets as a family?
2. How much debt is the family liable for?
3. Is there a will or estate plan in place?
4. Is there life insurance?
5. Who are the next of kin on record with bank accounts, emergency documents etc.?
6. What is each family member's financial responsibility?
7. What are common goals and expectations?

CHAPTER 10:
THE LONG GAME – INVESTING

"Omosede is super cool," Tsola had reassured Zuri when they'd talked about setting up the meeting to which she was currently headed. Still, as she waited for the elevator to take her to the seventeenth floor, she had to admit to herself that she was nervous. She had googled the girl and was slightly intimidated about what she had discovered about the young, brilliantly accomplished woman who'd agreed to speak with her about something that terrified her ever-so-slightly.

Omosede had an MBA from Stanford and a first degree from Oxford; she had worked for several investment banks and was, to put it mildly, a brain. As head of private banking at Concord Capital, her clients were typically high-net-worth individuals. Although the bank had a retail investment management arm that catered to the more modest income bracket Zuri belonged to, Omosede had agreed to have a chat with Zuri to point her in the right direction after a phone call with Tsola.

Zuri sat in the slightly chilly reception area, and glanced at her watch. *I hope this isn't going to be one of those meetings where you spend an hour waiting, only to spend fifteen minutes in actual conversation.* This was one of her pet peeves about working in Nigeria; zero respect for other people's time. She had been sent to Abuja once to meet with a prospective client, and he had told her to come at 10:00 a.m. insisting that she shouldn't be late, only to make her wait three hours for a meeting that took ten minutes—without so much as an apology.

She glanced around, noting the subtle-yet-high-end design of the space, when she saw a familiar statuesque, dark-skinned woman walking toward her with a big smile. She exuded an appealing confidence, kitted out in a striking dark pink knee-length dress, with a structured top section reminiscent of a dress from a recent Roland Mouret collection. It was a very unusual colour for a woman in finance to be rocking on a Wednesday; pink was not your typical go-to colour for women in her field. To crown her look was a gorgeous weave that was bone straight, dark and long enough that it was skimming her lower back. *Her hair's amazing. I wonder if it's Peruvian?*

"Hello, Zuri. Great to see you again," she greeted. "I hope you haven't been waiting long."

"Oh no, it's fine. I've barely been here five minutes. Thank you so much for taking the time to see me. I know you must be very busy."

"Oh it's fine! Anything for Tsola," Omosede replied with a slightly teasing smile. "Let's go into my office."

Zuri walked through the glass doors into Omosede's stunning workspace, dominated by white furniture with mustard-yellow accents. On her pale cream desk sat a mustard-coloured picture frames and ornaments. The sofa facing the window was gleaming white leather with ochre-yellow throw pillows. The view from the ceiling-to-floor windows showing off the Lagos skyline was absolutely breath-taking. *Omosede must be pretty important to her firm to have an office like this.*

"Tea? Coffee? Juice?" Omosede offered.

"No, thank you."

"Okay let's begin then," Omosede said as she gestured for Zuri to have a seat. "Tsola says you would like to start investing and want pointers as to how to get started."

Zuri nodded.

"Okay, so what's your investment history? What do you typically invest in? Stocks? Bonds?" Omosede asked.

Zuri took a deep breath. 'To be honest I'm a beginner—I've only ever invested in fixed deposits and never consistently. Even then it was only because I had a really pushy account officer who had targets to meet and convinced me to invest my Christmas bonus. But the interest is usually small and meaningless. So I'm like, *why bother*? When my five hundred thousand sits in the account for ninety days and all I have to show for it is a measly thirty thousand naira—what's the point?"

Omosede nodded knowingly as she jotted some notes down on a legal pad. "Don't worry, I know the kind you mean. The thing is, you have to have a more patient attitude to investing. The typical Nigerian is looking for that next big deal to make a killing. They want to 'hit', so if someone is talking to the about investment opportunities with a four percent return they say, 'what's the point? It's too small', but the point of that kind of investment is compounding interest—basically making interest on interest already earned. The key is to start early and stay consistent."

"That makes more sense. The interest earned is added to the original amount and earns interest of its own, and so on and so forth, right?" Zuri said contemplatively.

"Right. Obviously, there are other asset classes—better known as investments—that may have a higher return but with more risk. So I take it you've never invested in stocks before?" Omosede said with a wry smile.

"I've heard too many horror stories. In fact, my friend's father lost a lot of money in the Nigerian stock market in 2008 so I've always been too scared. The idea of stocks or bonds just sounds convoluted."

"They are really not as complex as you think, but I'll break it down as we go along." She leaned in conspiratorially. "Let me tell you a secret: the wealthiest people in the world make relatively simple investments. They typically invest in things that they understand, and it all boils down to what your goals are."

Zuri nodded. "That sounds like a great philosophy! Again, I really appreciate you taking the time out to speak to me."

"No problem. Let's establish a few things. What is your net worth?"

"Net worth?" Zuri looked puzzled. "I have absolutely no clue." *I think it's zero*, she thought, but she didn't want to say that out loud. "I earn about seven point two million naira per annum but I have no clue what my net worth is. Actually, no one has ever asked me that question. Isn't that a question reserved for people on the Forbes list like Dangote? Or at least people who are even remotely rich and have made some real money?"

Omosede smiled. "First of all, I want you to feel comfortable because everything we discuss here is confidential and there is absolutely no judgment, I promise. These questions are just so we have a starting point and can track your progress over time.

"I know people typically measure financial success by how much they earn—the income they get in salary from their job or business. However, your net worth is the true measure of how wealthy you are, because building wealth is ultimately not about how much you earn but how much of your income you are able to convert to assets that can provide you with an income in the future. Are you with me so far?" Omosede asked.

"Yes, I think so. So you mean how much of my income I can convert to assets like property and stocks. That kind of thing?" Zuri replied.

"Yes. Exactly," Omosede said

Zuri showed her frustration, with a situation that felt very unfair. "But property is so expensive. And stocks are so risky! For example, the flat I live in costs about seventy million and it would probably take me forever and a day to buy! This is the problem I've always had with all this investing stuff. It sounds good in theory, to say 'buy assets'. However, the reality is these assets are expensive! It's not as if it's beans to buy a house in Lekki Phase I," Zuri joked.

"Girl, slow your roll," Omosede smiled. "This is the part I find amusing. People will go from zero to a hundred in a flash. Lekki Phase I? You didn't even say Ikorodu! Let's just take baby steps and start with areas your income can support."

Zuri laughed too. "Right. Where should I start?"

"You work in real estate so you are aware of growth areas, like along the Lekki-Epe expressway. They are much more affordable and have immense growth potential. There are a few real estate companies we work with who offer payment plans for much cheaper real estate opportunities. Even though it's pretty far from the main city in terms of distance, that area is going to blow up in the next five to ten years."

Zuri hummed in agreement. It was a solid assessment.

"Anyway, we are skipping a few steps. We'll start with the basics. You earn seven point two million annually. What's your monthly income and how much disposable income do you have to invest?"

"I earn six hundred thousand a month after taxes, and I've been consistently setting aside twenty percent of my income for a few months. It's not a lot but what can I invest in?"

"You know, we offer investment products with entry points of as little as fifty thousand naira, so the amount is not a big issue. What's important at this stage is establishing your investment goals and devising an investment strategy that matches your goals," Omosede said. "There is no one-size-fits-all approach to investing. Everyone has different financial obligations, earning potential, and risk profiles."

Zuri held up her hands. "Now you've lost me! I'm not familiar with those terms."

"Let me give an example. Take two women say, Amaka and Chichi, who both earn two hundred thousand a month. Amaka has been saving fifty percent of her salary for the last three months and decides to invest in the stock market. She buys XYZ stock at one hundred and eighty-two naira per share and after a few months the stock price rose to two hundred and three. She is so excited that she shares the good news with Chichi. Chichi has been looking for ways to make money, outside of her salary, so she goes ahead and also invests the money she had been saving in XYZ stock.

"Most people tend to make the mistake of saying, *Mr Lagbaja made this investment and made a killing, so I'll make it too.* This 'me too' approach to making an investment decision is what often leads to a lot of people losing money, because they didn't take the time to really look at how they were investing. Amaka and Chichi may earn the same monthly salary but their circumstances are different.

"Amaka is twenty-five, lives with her parents, and has little or no obligations. Her expenses for the month mostly comprise of fuel for her car and credit for her phone.

"By choosing to buy stocks, she is buying equity or a fraction of ownership of the company. It's a relatively high-risk investment, but historically it gives better returns in the long run than other types of investments or asset class. The longer her money is invested, the higher the average rate of return. Since she has zero to no obligations and age is on her side, she can afford to take the risk of investing a huge portion of her earnings in the stock market in the long run. Clear so far?"

"Yes, it is."

Omosede continued, "Chichi, on the other hand, is thirty-two and married with two children under the age of seven. Her husband's income is inconsistent; therefore, she has a great deal of financial responsibility. She is partly responsible for paying rent and school fees. Chichi had been saving that money towards those payments, but was looking for "faster" ways to grow her money. This was a bad move because if the price of XYZ stock goes down, so will the value of her investment. Since she needed the money in the short-term, this was not a good investment to make for her situation."

Zuri realised what Omosede was trying to teach her. "I think I see where you are going with this. So basically what I invest in depends on why I'm investing and where I need to be with money and cash flow."

"Exactly. So let's talk a bit about what your investment goals are. Why do you want to invest?"

Zuri knew exactly what she wanted. The last few months had been a wakeup call. "I want financial security. I want the money I make to translate to something bigger in the future. And, I want to make enough money to maintain my lifestyle."

"You have to get a little bit more specific," Omosede said.

"Well, I'd like to own property and start building a stock portfolio, but I would also like to go on holiday. And I need a new car," Zuri rushed out in one breath.

Omosede smiled. "Here's the thing. You have to make choices, prioritise, and start slowly. Your resources are limited and you still have rent to pay. You'll eventually be able to do them all, but not all at once. For example, you probably can't afford to save and invest towards a car and a holiday at the same time on a salary of six hundred thousand, but we can start working towards those goals."

"Baby steps. Got it. So, how do I develop an investment strategy? It sounds complex."

"It really doesn't have to be. It's basically a fancy way of saying this is *how* you'll approach achieving your goals. It doesn't have to be complicated; you just set benchmarks. It could be as simple as saying to yourself, *I want to own property in the next five to ten years. I have found land that costs one million. So I will put twenty percent of my income in a money market fund towards reaching that goal. When I've bought the land, I'll start investing that twenty percent in a mix of stocks and treasury bills until I have two million to put towards developing the property.*"

Zuri was now officially an Omosede fan. "Can I just say I'm obsessed with you? You make this stuff so easy to understand."

She smiled at the compliment. "I try," Omosede said. "The thing is, ideally what we want long term is for you to build a diversified portfolio and decide your asset allocation."

"You've started with the finance speak again," Zuri said. "Break it down for a sister."

"Basically, long-term, we don't want you putting all your eggs in one basket, you ideally should have a mix of investments. For example, if the stock market isn't doing well, your investment in treasury bills—a less risky asset—give you access to more liquid assets. Liquid meaning you can more readily turn it into cash.

"Your asset allocation is basically a way of saying *this is the proportion of my income that will go in each asset class*. For example, A ratio of forty, twenty, twenty, twenty means forty percent in real estate, twenty percent each in treasury bills, stocks, and bonds."

"I think I get it, but what are the next steps?" Zuri asked.

"Well, I think you have some thinking to do, so I'll give you some forms to fill to determine your investment goals, your risk profile, how much you have available to invest and then we can develop an investment plan for you, and match your goals to some funds we have at Concord to help you achieve your goals."

Zuri settled in to her chair and filled the forms over the next hour, peppering Omosede with more questions.

It was one of the best things she'd ever done for herself.

* * *

As the Uber driver drove through the gates of Tsola's apartment building, Zuri wondered what exactly he had planned for the evening. She had sent him a text after her meeting with Omosede to say how excited she was about her investment goals and he had called her hours later suggesting that they celebrate over dinner at his, this evening.

She figured he was trying to make up for his absence because the last few weeks had been slightly tough on their relationship in terms of communication and spending time with each other. Tsola had just begun the intense-but-rewarding CEP course at Lagos Business School, meant for CEOs, Chairpersons and managing directors of businesses with an annual turnover of one billion naira and between fifty to a hundred employees. He was a huge proponent for self-development and was determined to get the best from the course but between classes, meetings, and work, they weren't getting a lot of "us" time.

She wasn't complaining either because she had been busy trying to get her money life together. After WIMBIZ, it had become apparent that she had to find ways to earn more, and her meeting with Omosede had only reinforced that. She had spent the last couple of weeks writing business plans and having strategy meetings with Mrs. Abafo-Williams to discuss how exactly to get started. Become an entrepreneur? Start a side business? Or seek a promotion at Richmond (which, to be perfectly blunt, she thought was highly unlikely, given the current economic situation).

As she rang the doorbell, the smell of food wafted from the kitchen. Had he ordered take out? Zuri wondered. Dominic, Tsola's cook from Coutonou made a mean beef in black pepper sauce, but the aroma something more sublime.

Tsola opened the door and gave her a kiss as she walked in. "Hello, darling! You are going to faint when you see the surprise I have for you."

He took her hand and led her through the living room to the terrace set up like it was straight out of a romance movie. Tea lights and candles were everywhere and in the centre stood a table for two with a stunning view of the Lekki-Ikoyi Bridge as a picturesque backdrop. In the middle was an ice bucket with a bottle of ice-cold Laurent-Perrier.

I could swear that is Chef Fregz standing over the table holding a menu, she thought as she walked towards the gorgeously set table. He was a Nigerian chef trained at Le Cordon Bleu in Paris and he did the most amazing things with traditional Nigerian food, giving them a modern twist. She low-key stalked him on Instagram.

Zuri turned to Tsola with a look of surprise on her face. "Tsola! Is that Chef Fregz?"

"Yup!" Tsola looked pleased. "I wanted to do something special for you and I know you are mildly obsessed with him and his food, Instagram stalker!" He teasingly poked her ribs.

"I know we haven't hung out properly in a few weeks but between LBS and the deals I'm trying to close, it's been hectic and there hasn't been a lot of time for us," Tsola said. "I wanted to make it up to you before you dump me."

Zuri turned, put her hands round him and smiled. "Easy tiger... it's not that serious. I've been busy too, so I get it."

"Plus, I'm so proud of all the steps you've been taking to improve your finances," said as he held her hand and headed to the table.

"Thanks babe," Zuri replied.

Chef Fregz returned to the table to present the evening's menu:

Cocoa and chili braised short ribs with sweet potato mash or the *jollof* bulgur and *ugu*. Dessert was a mango cheesecake with white chocolate cream and lime salted caramel. She was going to put on at least five pounds just thinking about it but for the slice of heaven that was Chef Fregz's food, it was SO worth it.

"So how was your meeting with Omo today?" Tsola asked.

"It was great! She was great." Zuri gushed. "I feel so much clearer about my goals. I think I'm going to start saving towards building a stock portfolio or maybe buy some land. I haven't decided yet. I just know I want to have an asset in place in the next twelve months."

"That's smart!"

"Yeah, I know," Zuri said, quite pleased with herself. "But I think I'm going to start saving towards buying a new car first though, this Uber life is getting expensive. It's great when it's once in a while, but I miss having my own car."

"Mmm, I get that. What kind of car though?" Tsola asked.
"I'm not sure, maybe a BMW like Lara. Not brand new, obviously, but something fairly used."

"Zuri. That's silly, you just got out of debt. You want to go back?"

His words touched a nerve. "How is that silly? Lara drives one and it's a great car."

"First of all, you are not Lara and you do not have Lara's income," Tsola said. "Secondly, Lara probably bought hers brand new or fairly used in America when the exchange rate was not what it is today."

Zuri began to get annoyed. "Yes I am aware I'm not Lara, but my income prospects are going to improve this year."

"That's exactly the problem. Wait till they improve first before you start investing in a luxury car. You'll just end up working for the car instead of the car working for you. Do you know how much it costs to fuel that car or replace the parts when there is a mechanical issue? You better ask Lara the cost of maintaining it and then double it because if you buy that car second hand in Nigeria, it will be at the mechanic's shop every other month.

"I really don't understand why people do this; why not buy a car your income can support. I'm sure you can save towards a brand new Toyota and the parts are easier to replace. Or do you want to go back to being broke? Me? I don't date broke women. I've done the whole date-the-broke-and-beautiful-girl thing in the past and it's not cute."

Zuri was livid. "I don't understand why you are speaking to me as if I'm a child. This conversation is frankly very disrespectful, but it's not your fault. It's because I was open and honest about my problems from the get go.

"Broke and beautiful, *abi*? Is that how you see me, Tsola? I have no words."

"Calm down Zuri. Maybe that came out wrong, but I just don't want you going down the wrong path." Tsola had begun to realise she was upset.

"A car is a depreciating asset, didn't Omo explain that to you? Once you drive it, it begins to lose value, so it makes no sense spending all your income trying to maintain a car your current salary can't support," Tsola tried to explain.

Zuri was not having it, and shut the conversation down. "Listen, it's enough. I don't want to talk about this anymore. I'm just going to order an Uber to take me home as soon as we are done eating. Thank you for dinner. It's lovely."

"I'll drop you at home," Tsola said.

"No thanks. I need to be alone," Zuri replied.

They ate in silence for the rest of the meal.

SMART MONEY LESSON:
A FEW THINGS TO CONSIDER BEFORE
YOU POP YOUR INVESTING CHERRY

The world of investing might seem daunting, but like learning a new skill, it takes time and patience to understand. Here are my thoughts on how to start investing in Nigeria.

Know Your Asset Classes/Types of Investments

Stocks: I can't count the number of times I've heard 'I don't do stocks'. Granted, the level of risk involved is not for everyone but the stock market can be your friend, especially if you are young. The Nigerian stock market lists stocks of some of the best companies this country has to offer and the criteria that has to be met for companies to be listed mean that they have been thoroughly vetted, so they have corporate governance and audited accounts. If you can take the risk of investing in your friend's fish farm, you can take the risk of investing some of your long-term savings in the stock market.

The saying 'No one ever got rich from a savings account' holds true now more than ever, because the value of cash decreases over time due to inflation, currently about 15% in Nigeria. It is important to understand that even though stocks are volatile in the short run, they've historically risen in value in the long term.

I am passionate about the growth prospects of the Nigerian stock market. I believe it is a solid platform to build long-term wealth. In the words of Warren Buffet when it comes to investing in stocks, "Be fearful when others are greedy and greedy only when others are fearful." Since people are wary of the Nigerian stock market, it is a good time to research and invest in good companies that are undervalued.

I do not believe in borrowing money to buy stock, nor do I believe that the stock market is a money doubling scheme, which was the motivation for many people's investments in 2007, when the market was at its peak. That is an easy way to get burnt, but I believe in systematically using money you can afford to forget about to build long-term wealth. i.e. money you would have used to go shopping or buy credit for the month, not your money for rent or school fees.

The cardinal rule when you invest is, *don't invest in anything you don't understand.* You should always do some research, ask some questions. Here are a few tips to get started:

- *Subscribe to proshare (www.proshareng.com).*
- *Pick a few stocks from different sectors to research.*
- *What do you like about the companies as businesses? What are the fundamentals behind them?*
- *What are the growth prospects of the company in the current economic climate? Do they have any durable competitive advantage?*

- *Do some research on the companies past performance, historic price, dividend yield, and liquidity of the stocks?*
- *Speak to an investment adviser or stockbroker about your findings.*

Real estate: An investment in real estate in Nigeria is mostly always a good idea. It's a great long-term investment with medium risk, decent cash flows and a reasonable expectation of an increase in value, especially in growth areas. Real estate investments include residential rental property, raw land, or commercial (business) real estate.

An investment in real estate does have some distinct risks. It is possible for property values to go down as well as up, so you could lose some of your investment principal (the initial amount of money invested). Most of all, real estate is not a "liquid" investment—it may be hard to sell the property when you want to, leaving your money tied up when you need it.

That said, real estate is a great asset to have and most people know this, but are deterred from entering the market either because they think it's too expensive or are waiting to 'hit' so they can build their own house to live in. However, it's better to find something that's in your price range and just START!

Mutual funds: A mutual fund is an investment vehicle that is made up of a pool of funds collected from many investors for the purpose of investing in securities such as stocks, bonds, money market instruments and similar assets. Mutual funds are operated by money/fund managers, who invest the fund's capital and attempt to produce capital gains and income for the fund's investors.

The advantage of this is that an investor no longer has to worry about the day-to-day administrative issues that come with making investment decisions as this is passed on to a professional fund manager. It gives small investors access to a professionally managed diversified portfolio. Mutual funds in Nigeria are mostly open-ended and affordable, which mean that you can start with as little as ten thousand naira and liquidate at market value when you want to.

Money market instruments (i.e. Treasury bills): Money market instruments are basically short-term securities like treasury bills (money you lend to the government) or commercial paper (money lent to institutions). Treasury bills are more common and arguably more secure.
You cannot bid directly for treasury bills; you have to go through a broker, your bank or a finance house. Nigerian treasury bills are usually sold bi-weekly, and upcoming primary auctions are usually reported in the financial section of national newspapers. The CBN also publishes a quarterly treasury bills auction calendar on their website. The interest rate is not fixed but fluctuates based on demand (volume of bids) and supply (amount offered by

the central bank).

Alternatively, you can look into investing in a money market fund. This is a specific type of mutual fund that invests in money market securities. It preserves your capital, pays you a return that's comparable to prevailing money market rates in Nigeria

Establish Your Investment Goals

The crucial question is, why are you investing? This may be a more difficult question to answer than many people realise, because they haven't fully articulated what they want their money to do for them. Are you putting money aside toward rent? A car? Retirement? Building assets? The reason you are investing will determine what kind of investments you make.

For example, if you were investing towards your rent next year, the worst thing you can do is say, "Let me invest my savings each month in the stock market." Stocks can be very volatile and your capital might be lower in value when you need it the most. A money market product or treasury bills might be a better option. However, if you were working a nine-to-five job and were saving towards a business you plan to start in five to ten years, then the stock market could be an option.

There are no right or wrong answers. Your investment goals should reflect your financial obligations, what you value most, and what you want the money you make to be able to do for your life in general.

Develop an Investment Strategy

It is important to write down your investment strategy to clearly articulate your thoughts. Once your strategy is written, you should ensure it matches your long-term investment goals. Writing down your strategy gives you a plan/guide to refer back to in times of chaos and help you avoid making emotional decisions. It also gives you something to review and change if your investment goals change or you start earning more money.

It doesn't have to be complicated. Even if you think what you have to start with is too little, begin with a savings account and start building it up. You can give yourself benchmarks

Here is an example.

Ivie
Goal: Buy land
20% of salary deposited in savings account until ₦200,000 is saved
Take ₦200,000 and split: ₦100,000 for fixed deposits, ₦100,000 for stock portfolio. Repeat until fixed deposits reach target amount.
When fixed deposits = ₦1 – 1.5 million range, buy land in Awoyaya.

If possible, sit down with an investment advisor and discuss those goals and financial obligations you've mapped out so that they can match your goals with the investment products or asset classes best suited to your lifestyle.

If your goal is to build a house in five to ten years and your financial obligations include paying children's school fees and rent, you will want an investment advisor to match your goals with products and asset classes that will help you attain them.

Determine Your Risk Profile

When people ask me about investing, one of the most recurrent themes is the need for high returns. "My money is in my savings account and it's giving me little interest. What can I invest in that will keep my money safe but grow it very fast?" It doesn't work that way. You can't have both low risk and high returns. Simply, a lower risk investment has lower potential for profit. A higher risk investment has a higher potential for profit but also a potential for a greater loss.

You've heard that saying, 'No risk, no reward'? There is a strong correlation between risk and return. The investments that offer the highest return in the long run also come alongside a healthy measure of risk. For example, if you have one hundred thousand naira and you put it in a savings account, treasury bills or buy XYZ stock. Chances are in ten years your XYZ stock (through capital appreciation and dividend yield) will be worth more than savings or treasury bills. However, because stocks are volatile in nature your XYZ stocks could also be worth less.

A **conservative investor's** primary objective is to preserve the capital and receive regular income. They have a low tolerance for risk and hence a major chunk of their investment would be allocated to debt or money market mutual funds.

A **moderately aggressive investor** is the one who is willing to take controlled risk for moderate returns. Such investors are generally recommended a mix of balanced portfolios.

Aggressive investors consider risk as an opportunity and leverage their experience and knowledge to take intelligent financial decisions. The major share of their investment, therefore, goes to growth and equity schemes.

Pick an Investment Firm

Now, you are ready to invest! Doing your own preliminary research on what investment options are available to you in Nigeria is great but the reality is no matter how skilled you are in your business or line of work, you may not have the skill or patience required to pick the best investments for your situation. It's important to speak to a professional to guide you. Commercial banks offer some great savings products but an investment firm gives you a wider range of investment options that include stocks, bonds, real estate and other investment opportunities.

At this point, you should have a clearer idea of what your investment goals are, your financial obligations, how much you have in your budget to invest and a fair idea of your risk profile. With all of this, I think you are armed with enough information to begin a conversation with an investment professional.

Knowing what you want to achieve is key so that nobody can '*wele*' you into investing in products or assets that are not in line with your goals. Even though they are professionals, don't let them dismiss your concerns or questions. Whether you are investing one hundred naira or one hundred million, *na* your money! You have every right to ask questions, and you should. Remember the cardinal rule: do not invest in things you don't understand.

MOMENT OF TRUTH

Some investment firms will try to sell you on a product that might not be right for your particular financial situation based on their own self-interest (if for example they have a mandate to sell the rights issue for a particular stock or they are getting commission from selling a particular product). This is why it is extremely important to be clear on your own investment goals and why you are investing in the first place, so they can appropriately match your goals to the products they have available. Make sure you choose a firm with a track record and an investment advisor you can honestly talk to about your financial situation.

Knowing what you want to achieve is key so that nobody can *'wele'* you into investing in products or assets that are not in line with your goals. Even though they are professionals, don't let them dismiss your concerns or questions. Whether you are investing one hundred naira or one hundred million, *na* your money! You have every right to ask questions, and you should. Remember the cardinal rule: do not invest in things you don't understand.

QUESTIONS YOU SHOULD ASK YOUR INVESTMENT ADVISOR

INVESTMENT STRATEGY

What is their asset allocation strategy? what will they be investing your money in, stocks? Bonds? Real estate? How diversified is the investment/fund/product? What is the asset allocation mix/ratio (i.e. the product invests in stocks, bonds, real estate and treasury bills proportions for example, 10:20:40:30)?

RISK

Talk to them about how much risk you are willing to take on. With some investments there is a possibility of losing a portion of your principal. Although the returns on these types of investments attract better returns, ask yourself if your lifestyle would change if the value of your principal investment went down. This would determine how much risk appetite you have.

PROFITABILITY

What are your expected returns on the investment? Are the returns guaranteed or is there a possibility of a reduction if the market conditions change?

LIQUIDITY

How much access do you have to the money invested? So if you decided to liquidate the investment prematurely, will there be any penalties? If so, how much?

> **TENOR**
>
> How long is your money locked in for? You don't want to invest money you may need soon in a long-term instrument.

CHAPTER 11:
EARNING MORE

As Zuri waited patiently for a waiter to bring a menu to the table, she gazed out the window to admire the people eating by the poolside at the George Hotel; it had gorgeous grounds, and it was a nice day. The idea of sitting outside was tempting but she knew that despite the canopies that covered the tables, in a matter of hours the heat would become unbearable and the flies that were sure to follow the food would make matters worse. She decided it was best to stay indoors under the protection of the air conditioning.

As she perused the menu, trying to decide what drink to order before the rest of the girls joined her for brunch, her mind drifted to the dramatic events over the last couple of months.

Six months ago, Mr Okeke causing a scene in her building over the debt she owed was the most embarrassing thing she thought could happen to anyone she knew. She now realised how naïve she had been. Still, the last few months had shown her the resilience of herself and her friends, Adesuwa and Ladun especially. Both were going through things that would break most people, but she had watched both women handle their issues with true grit and an unimaginable amount of grace.

Adesuwa was a trooper. Not many women would be able to handle the fact that their husband had ended their marriage via text message. After weeks of being missing in action and cleaning out their joint account, the coward had sent a rubbish text message to explain. He told her he was tired of being married and needed a fresh start. He had found the love of his life and was moving to London to pursue a business opportunity—a club! Adesuwa had been inconsolable for weeks.

After the shock had worn off and the reality of her financial situation had set in, she began to pick up the pieces. She started by liquidating what was left of Soji's failing ventures, restructured the loans with the banks, set up meetings to agree to a repayment plan that was achievable, and sold some off the assets she owned to pay down part of the debt, so she could buy some goodwill. Still, she was facing a long journey to escape the financial mess. Zuri was in awe of how Adesuwa had transformed herself into a Wonder Woman in a matter of months, taking charge of her own destiny.

Ladun on the other hand, although removed from the day-to-day dealings of tackling the Ashoni family's financial woes, had surprised everyone with the grace with which she had handled the drastic adjustments. They had moved to a much smaller flat in Lekki that was closer to Ajah than to Phase I. Her kids had moved to a new school at the end of the previous term and she was currently looking for work and exploring business ideas that would help her earn extra income while Bode and his brothers soldiered on in the fight with the banks.

Zuri was forced back to reality by the sound of Tami's excited voice. "*Ah ah.* Where *you dey go?* "Face beat" and everything. I thought it was just brunch with the girls?"

Tami looked very pleased with herself. "My highlight is popping, *abi*? I got my makeup done by Anita Brows. I'm going to "le boo's" dad's sixtieth birthday, and you know we have to slay."

"Anyway, you are not going to believe what I'm about to tell you!" Tami said as she plonked her Chanel bag on the table carelessly and settled in the seat closest to the window.

"What? Although, to be honest, I'm not really interested. Please pass the juice."

"You are so annoying, but I'm going to tell you anyway," Tami said. "I know who Soji's side piece is!"

"Really? Who? How do you know? Do we know her?" Zuri knew she wasn't making any sense but Tami had the answer to question that had been plaguing them for months.

"Chinasa!" Tami exclaimed. "You know how she's always *forming* 'big brother, little sister' with Soji and all his friends? It turns out she's been sleeping with Soji this entire time."

"Chinasa, *ke*? How? But she's so young! Are you sure? Where did you hear this?"

"A client that just left my studio spilled the beans. One Tosin, apparently, who used to be "BFFs" with her," Tami said using air quotes for emphasis. "I think they fought, so now she's telling everyone the girl's business. Tosin even showed me pictures on WhatsApp to prove it. "

Zuri's jaw dropped. "You can't be serious!"

"Oh, it gets worse! You remember how I told you that Seni Foster was dating Amanda from high school? And that he had bought her a flat in London and all that?"

Zuri nodded.

"Chinasa is also all up in that mix. She showed me pictures on WhatsApp of Chinasa in Paris, getting off Seni's private plane, eating at restaurants and coming out of hotels. So while that *mumu* Soji thinks he has found the love of his life and is spending Adesuwa's hard earned money to impress her, Chinasa has a sugar daddy that is keeping her in Gucci and gold."

"Does Adesuwa know?"

"If she doesn't, she will soon hear. That Tosin girl is telling everyone!"

Zuri stared at Tami in bewilderment, still trying to process the information. "What I don't understand is, she's young and educated. Why can't she find someone her own age and unmarried? Chinasa is what, twenty-three, twenty-four? She's from a wealthy family, so she can't even use hunger as an excuse for her behaviour. But I don't blame her alone.

"And why a loser like Soji? He has no money of his own. I mean, with Seni Foster the motives are clear—he may be a zero in the looks department but I would imagine that dating him came with perks—plane tickets, fancy hotels, designer bags and an allowance."

Tami laughed. "Yup! I've heard he's quite generous. Soji though...," she shook her head. "That remains a mystery."

They both looked up to see Lara walk across to their table by the pool in her immaculate all-white ensemble.

"Hello darlings," she said as she hugged and gave each of them a kiss before taking her seat. "What were you guys talking about?" Lara asked looking at both girls suspiciously.
She shook her head in disbelief as Tami filled her in.

"I wish I could say I was surprised, but I'm not. I've been saying this thing about this Chinasa for some time now. I never bought into her whole *I'm an innocent girl* routine. It was too convenient how she seemed to be every popular guy's little sister and such good friends with their wives, it was only a matter of time before she slept with one of them."

"Let's change the subject, *jo*. I don't even want to be caught having this conversation about Adesuwa's marriage," Zuri said. "*My hand no dey.*"

Tami laughed. "Moving on! You know what I've been thinking? Between listening to Omosede at WIMBIZ and watching Adesuwa and Ladun walk through fire, I woke up! When it's close to home like this, it makes you realise that if you are not on top of your money you can be blindsided at any time."

"Tell me about it," Lara said. "Ladun's situation made me start checking myself. She went from calling me about getting the numbers of personal shoppers on Instagram so she could get a new Hermes bag, to calling to ask about advice on whether she should focus on her business ideas or job interviews. Anyway, I sent her to look at resources at She Leads Africa."

"*Mehn*, she asked me too and I couldn't answer. A few months ago I would have told her to become an entrepreneur, easy peasy, but I'm starting to learn that this entrepreneurship life is not for everyone," said Tami.

"*Ah ah now*, what do you mean by that? Ladun has skills, she just needs time to figure things out," Zuri said.

"No, I know she has skills, I wasn't even trying to throw shade!" Tami replied seriously. "I'm just speaking from my recent experience. All these years I've been deceiving myself that I am an entrepreneur but I've just been playing at a hobby. It wasn't until I set up a meeting with that Bimbo babe that I met at WIMBIZ from Audeo the accounting firm, that I realised my business had actually been running at a loss."

"Really?" Zuri looked shocked.

"I could see that happening actually," Lara said knowingly as she sipped her tea. "What? It's true, *na*! To the trained eye it was obvious to see you didn't have a proper business model! You were probably just spending your cash flows as if they were your profits."

"As in, Lara, I really want to abuse you right now but that's exactly what Bimbo said when she helped me clean up my books," Tami said sheepishly. "I'm ashamed to say I never kept any proper financial records. No balance sheet, no cash flow and no profit and loss statement. And I've been *shining teeth* for five years saying, 'Hello! I'm an entrepreneur'."

Zuri and Lara cracked up.

"The funny thing is, it's actually not that hard!" Tami continued. "I don't need to become an accountant. I've just learnt to interpret the numbers and what they mean for my business. Now I'm clearer on how the business is really doing, and how exactly it works. I've put myself on a salary to stop mixing my business and personal finances. You guys, I don't know how I've stayed afloat this long."

"Your rich daddy!" Lara coughed.

Zuri started laughing so hard she wanted to cry. "But it's true, sha, Lara is right! You have always had several cushions. Your daddy or whichever boy is toasting you at the moment."

"I'm not even going to lie, until recently, I just thought I never had to worry about money, I would just go from my daddy's house to my rich husband's house," Tami laughed.

"Who didn't know?" Lara said cheekily.

"Don't get it twisted. I still want to marry a rich husband but now I'm clear about who I want to be," Tami said.

Lara and Zuri exchanged knowing glances and collapsed into another round of laughter.

"Who, *abeg*?" Zuri asked.

"The new trophy wife," Tami responded.

"A what? There are different types of trophy wives now?"

Tami rolled her eyes. "I was reading a Huffington Post article that said the term 'trophy wife' has been upgraded to version two point zero. She is now a woman who is making good money and is in a position of power, à la Amal Clooney."

"I love it!" Zuri said. "We need to go hard and figure out to make this money, ladies. After my meeting with Omosede a few weeks ago, I realised I wasn't making enough money and I need to find more ways to earn. Multiple streams of income, guys! Multiple streams of income!"

"So true!" Lara said. "My passive income game is up these days. I feel like my stockbroker and real estate agent are my *bestos* these days because I talk to them every other week."

"*Ah ah*, check you out!" Tami laughed.

"I'm serious, now that the economy is slow, assets are relatively cheap, so I set aside at least twenty percent of my income every month towards any real estate or stock market opportunities that come my way from those two because they are the best. They get it. I can hook you up if you want."

"I'm a little obsessed with Omosede at the moment because we are on track to reaching my investment goals but I'm open to listening to what other opportunities your guys have," Zuri replied.

"Awwww! Yay for us! We need to keep ourselves accountable," Tami said earnestly. "We would never let each other get fat, so let's never let each other get broke!"

Zuri was glad her conversations with the girls had evolved from just gossiping and talking about clothes to discussing business and opportunities to earn. There was now a balance.

Her mentor, Mrs Abafo-Williams had shared something profound with her the other day that had stuck. *You are the average of the five people you spend the most time with. If you hang out with four broke people you will be the fifth, and if you hang out with four business minded people, you will be the fifth.* Zuri had been amused, but the statement had more than a ring of truth to it. She was fast realising that terrible money habits could be formed by just the people you chose to hang out with—even if they were great. If one friend talked about her business and investments, others in the group would likely start speaking about theirs too.

Her thoughts were interrupted by the sound of her phone buzzing. It was Tsola again, and she wasn't in the mood to speak to him. She was still upset at how harsh he had been to her, and she wasn't sure she could be with someone so judgmental.

"Who is that?" Lara asked.

"Tsola." She replied flatly.

"You're still not talking to him? *My friend*, get real! You know that you cannot afford that car and he was only telling you the truth."

"*Abeg, abeg.* Stay out of it."

* * *

Back in her apartment, Zuri stared at her computer as she went over the notes for her pitch to Mr Tunde in the morning. Even though she had barely been able to practice her pitch with the girls over brunch because of all the gossip, she was pretty confident he would be impressed.

Her mind wandered back to their conversation at brunch. She wasn't a hypocrite, so she recognised that she certainly wanted all the things Chinasa and her friends lusted after too, but the question was, at what cost?

It wasn't news to Zuri that if she wanted to reach her goals and eventually live the life she wanted, she had to earn more money. She couldn't even front, she wanted that 'PJ lifestyle' as much as the next girl. In this generation, where almost everyone was a hustler in one capacity or the other, she didn't know many people who weren't aspiring to that lifestyle, from the corporate execs to the entrepreneurs. As a matter of fact, according to Instagram these days, everyone was a CEO raking in millions of naira from their businesses.

She remembered a time she had hankered for that life so much that she even entertained the idea of a sugar daddy because the pressure to keep up in Lagos was intense, but thankfully, her better self had prevailed. She liked designer things as much as the next girl but at what cost? Some prices were too high.

She knew she wanted to make more money but meeting some of the women at WIMBIZ had given her the wakeup call she needed. She was now more aware of the kind of woman she wanted to be. Yes, she wanted more money but she also wanted to drive impact. The experience made her realise that she wasn't doing enough with her life or maximising her potential; some of those women had started out small but each of them was making a positive impact in their industries and for Zuri, the connecting thread had been purpose and passion. These were women who felt connected to their purpose in life and were fully engaged in the work that they did every day. She wanted to feel that. She wanted to put herself in a position to earn more but to also create value that would make a positive impact.

Weeks after the WIMBIZ conference, she had toyed with the idea of becoming an entrepreneur and starting her own business but after an eventful brunch meeting with Mrs Abafo-Williams (Mrs A to her mentees), who had been assigned as her mentor, her thoughts on that had changed. They had met up for coffee a few weeks ago, and she had told Zuri to come ready to talk about her goals.

They'd met at Cactus, mid-morning on a very wet Thursday. Zuri had arrived twenty minutes early; she understood the value of Mrs A's time and hadn't wanted to risk being late.

After she had pitched summaries of the business ideas she had been working on, Mrs A poked holes in each one, asking questions about proof of concept, customer acquisition strategies and scalability, none of which Zuri could answer. She was about to give up when Mrs A explained something profound to her.

"You know, leveraging on your skill-set to maximise your earning potential doesn't have to mean starting your own business, right?" Mrs A said with concern. 'The fact is not everyone is an entrepreneur—it's more important to be entrepreneurial in your thinking and to find ways to add value wherever you are."

At the time Zuri had wanted to object because she felt like she would be excluded from the new elite—young entrepreneurs who were developing new ideas and creating a new world. Did Mrs A think she wasn't cut out for business?

As though sensing her concerns, Mrs A said, "Don't worry—it's not that I'm saying you won't be good at business, I'm just pointing out the fact that there are other options. You sound so passionate when you are describing the work that you do at Richmond, and all the changes you would make if you were in charge that I think there's still room for growth there. Trust me when I say you can start a business in any phase of your life. There's no rush! The key is to only pursue the ideas that keep you up at night. You do not seem overly excited about any of the ideas you've pitched to me today. So my suggestion is focus on expanding your role at Richmond because you are passionate about the work you do there, you've just gotten bored with the role you've been saddled with. Am I right?"
Zuri nodded.

"So have you spoken to your boss about expanding your role?" Mrs A asked.

"No! Because they'll never go for it. They are sacking people right now and I'm barely out of probation. No one will listen to me," Zuri said

"You think no one will listen to you, but you would be surprised! If you don't ask, the answer will always be no. But first you need to figure out what you are asking for in detail. I told you before that in every crisis there is opportunity. So how are you best placed to serve the company in its present circumstance?"

"I'm not sure," Zuri confessed. "I had pitched an idea about creating a brand new division to my immediate supervisor, Mr Obi, about a year ago but he basically laughed in my face and told me to get serious. To be honest he was probably right, I don't have enough experience to start a new division. I still think it's a great idea but I'm not sure I have what it takes to execute."

Mrs A then told her frankly, "Women have what is called 'Imposter Syndrome'. We tend to rate ourselves lower than the rest of the world rates us. If I asked you to rate yourself on a scale of one to ten when it comes to how capable you are to create and run the division you are proposing, what would you say?"

"A four or five... maybe?"

"If I gave your male counterpart with exactly the same skill set and experience than you, he would probably give himself an eight because he is more confident, and men tend to over-estimate their expertise and then figure it out later."

Zuri had known this was true. Her colleague, Tobe, would volunteer for a task immediately it was suggested while she sat there second-guessing herself, but then always asked for her help later when it came to execution.

Mrs A looked at her pointedly then said, "This is my advice. Don't give up! Go back and dissect your idea, put it back together again and then re-present it, but this time to Mr Tunde. He sounds like he's tough but an ally, so he might be of help.

"The point of every business is to make a profit. That's the bottom line. To make profit your idea must either be generating more revenue for the company or reducing costs. However, if I'm honest, it'll be an easier sell if it's generating more revenue for the firm because what managers want to hear is how to make more money—they see cost cutting ideas as part of your job anyway, so it won't sound revolutionary to them even if it is.

"The thing is, when you have to prove the value of your ideas by persuading other people to buy into it; it clears up your thinking. So I want you to go back and think about that idea. How can it create the most value for your company in a cost effective way, given the state of the economy? Then poke holes in your argument. What are the reasons Mr Tunde might come up with to suggest it won't work? Find ways to counter the other side of the argument. And I implore you; use numbers to illustrate your points. The numbers never lie and once a reasonable person sees in black and white that an idea is financially feasible, that you have taken the time to do your research and have the passion and confidence to execute, there's no reason they should say no. Even if they do, don't give up just find a way to reframe the problem, make your argument stronger and re-present it. Once Mr Tunde says yes, you can find a reasonable way to tie in your own compensation. If it's tied to performance it will be a relatively easy sell."

That was three weeks ago. Zuri had left the meeting excited. She felt like it was the ginger she needed to get herself in gear.

As Zuri knocked on Mr Tunde's door and waited, she took a shaky breath. She believed in her idea; she knew it could work but she wasn't sure if the bureaucracy at Richmond would give it a chance. Mr Tunde was more open-minded than most of the management team but he was very old-school and was steadfast in his beliefs about how things should be done.

I'm not going to allow fear or negative thoughts to overwhelm me, Zuri thought.

She walked in confidently as she mentally went over her notes and the order she was going to present the information.

"Morning Zuri, take a seat," Mr Tunde said as he observed her sceptically and gestured to the chair in front of his table.

"Morning, Mr Tunde," Zuri smiled as she sat down. "Thank you again for agreeing to block out this time in your schedule to have this meeting with me. I truly appreciate it."

"That's alright. So what's this fantastic idea you have come up with?"

Zuri spent almost an hour with him first going over the idea of a value-add online marketplace for their clients to meet curated, well-vetted interior designers with a furniture component. Then, he probed some of the pros and cons of the idea, looking for weak spots and questioning the numbers she presented. Zuri knew her stuff. She gave all the right answers and he was impressed about how thorough her research was.

"I'm so glad you like the idea, sir. I know with your backing we will succeed. That's why I'd like to discuss a different compensation structure," Zuri said.

"The current structure at Richmond is to pay monthly salaries and then give a thirteenth month salary bonus, but I would like to suggest an extra commission based compensation for this division," she continued.

"I knew there had to be a catch," Mr Tunde replied. "We have had to let go of staff recently, so clearly we don't have money to pay commission."

"I understand Mr Tunde but what I'm asking is performance based and it would only start after the third month of operation when we've started seeing the profits," Zuri said. "Every month we exceed a thirty-six percent profit margin, I would like a point five percent of the profits raked in by my division to be paid to us. Point two-five percent should be reinvested in the division to fund new experimental ideas, and another point two-five towards compensating the team for their hard work. I would also like a twenty percent increase in my own salary if this idea works and is profitable by the third month."

Mr Tunde looked at her. "Why thirty-six?" He asked.

"Because I know that when business is good, we typically make that amount from our other income streams, so if I manage to exceed that percentage, I think it's fair to get compensated for it."

Mr Tunde stared at her or a few seconds then said, "I have to give it to you, you thought this one through and it sounds like you've set very high performance goals for yourself, so I'll tell you now that I like the idea but I have to run it by the rest of the partners and get back to you. It shouldn't be a problem because it's all contingent on you making us more money. If you can't deliver, then we don't have to pay you and if you deliver it's a win-win. This is a great initiative Zuri. I'm honestly proud of you."

***

It had been a triumphant day. She thought about all the anxiety on

the lead up to the meeting with Mr Tunde, but in the end, it was all worth it. She felt she was ready to crush this new challenge. As she stared at the screen of her phone, she realised that the first person she wanted to share this accomplishment with was Tsola. She had practised her pitch on him so many times for the last few weeks—before their big fight—and he'd been absolutely supportive, giving her pointers.
It took everything in her not to pick up her phone and call him to give him a blow-by-blow account of what had happened in her meeting with Mr Tunde.

Her doorbell rang. She looked through the peephole to see Tsola standing there. And for some reason, she couldn't stop smiling. She took a deep breath, trying to compose herself before she opened the door.

"I'm sorry," he said as the door swung open. "I hope these make up for it. I didn't know what kind of flowers you liked. So I just told them to make me something beautiful." He stepped aside to reveal a flower arrangement.

Zuri smiled. They were beautiful. "They're gorgeous. I love them! Thank you." She hesitated. "Would you like to come in?" she invited.

"No. I just came to drop the flowers. Of course I want to come in!" he joked, breaking the tension. "But you're a stubborn girl, sha. I know I was a bit harsh but not picking up my phone calls for a week?"
"A bit? You were waaaay judgmental."

"Judgmental? I still stand by my point, but the way I communicated it was not great."

"Whatever."

"You know I'm right."

As she looked around for a vase, she noticed an envelope tucked into the flowers. "*Ah ah,* did you write me a love letter?"

Tsola smiled.

She opened the envelope. It had two tickets to Cape Town, South Africa.

SMART MONEY LESSON: MAXIMISE YOUR EARNING POTENTIAL BY FOCUSING ON FINDING YOUR PURPOSE

Nine out of ten times when people ask how they can make more money my answer is find your purpose. Yes, it sounds trite, but this is a basic truth.

Your purpose is your calling; the thing that drives you to be successful because it is what you were created to do. It sits at the centre of three aspects of your life:

Skill-set. The things that you are good at, either because it's what you've studied or something you've spent hours honing.

Passion. People often confuse this with the things they like doing. It is that idea that burns deep inside you, so much so that you can't stop thinking about it until you execute. I like to say it makes you feel like you are pregnant with ideas.'

Earning potential. Your idea has to solve a problem that people will be willing to pay for.

People are complex, so it's possible to be called to several things, or for your purpose to evolve. An article written by Fred Swaniker of the African Leadership Group explains purpose best: to determine if something is your purpose, it must answer three questions. "Is it big enough (Which speaks to impact)? Are you in a unique position to make it happen (What skills or resources do you have or have access to execute the idea)? And are you passionate enough about it (does it pass the sleepless night test)?" He explains that if the answer is yes to all three, then it is probably your calling.

When it comes to earning money it's important for people to understand purpose because, they often pursue an idea and then can't follow through on because they haven't thought through those three questions.

You can earn money from a side business, side deals, investing, and passive income but ultimately the mechanism with which you primarily and actively earn an income plays a huge role in determining how wealthy you become. The more money you can generate from the mechanism you choose, will determine how much you have to invest in a side business, stocks etc.

So how do you earn more? The most popular answer these days is become an entrepreneur, start your own business. I have seen lots of articles and memes on Instagram and Twitter that say, 'If you don't follow your dreams, you'll end up working for someone who did', which is fair enough, if a bit of an over-generalisation.

In order to maximise your earning power and have the ability to invest, you need to pursue a career you are passionate about and create multiple streams of income. This does not necessarily mean you have to become an entrepreneur. The reality is, not everyone is cut out to be their own boss and you need to learn this early on. Being a boss is not about working for yourself and avoiding the discipline of a nine-to-five.

There are two ways to be stuck (and you don't want to be stuck in your thirties or forties):
1) Stuck in a 9-5 job you hate, and
2) Stuck in an entrepreneurial role you cannot handle.

Are We Glamorising Entrepreneurship?

Just ten to fifteen years ago in Africa, becoming financially successful and making your parents proud generally meant that you had to become a doctor, lawyer, engineer, accountant and maybe even an investment banker. Pursuing a university degree then deciding to become an entrepreneur would have caused mayhem in most Nigerian homes. You were expected to choose a profession, work hard at it, then scale the career ladder to success. However, with the scarcity of 'good' jobs and unemployment on the rise, starting a business has become the new normal for many graduates. In fact, entrepreneurship has become one of the most sustainable ways to solve Africa's unemployment problem. However, are we glamorising it to the detriment of our long-term success?

Three things we should probably reconsider:

1. Selling the idea that entrepreneurship is the ONLY guaranteed way to success

I can't count the number of times I've heard, 'If you don't follow your dreams, you'll end up working for someone who did' or 'No one ever got rich working a nine-to-five'. These are overgeneralisations that have consequences because the fact is, not everyone is cut out to be an entrepreneur. Plus, if we all become our own bosses who is going to work for whom? Who will be the employees?

It is wonderful that non-traditional avenues to earn money have opened up in the form of entrepreneurship, but why do we always have to have two extremes? Mark Zuckerberg is the founder of Facebook, but Sheryl Sandberg Facebook's COO and author of 'Lean In' (which has helped millions of women around the world in the work place) is not just an employee. Just because she isn't the founder of Facebook it doesn't make her less important because she focuses on being a value-driven individual. To paraphrase Dustin Moskovitz, if you joined Facebook as employee number one thousand, you would still have made roughly twenty million dollars.

Shouldn't the focus be on encouraging people to be entrepreneurial in their thinking whether they work in a corporation or run their own business? People who are entrepreneurial in their thinking are value-driven. They adopt critical thinking and embrace innovation and continuous improvement. They are the ones you see solving problems every day and are getting paid to do so regardless of whether they are the founders of the company or not.

2.   *Are we choosing entrepreneurship for the right reasons?*

With entrepreneurship growing in global popularity, everyone wants to be a boss. Many graduates don't even bother joining the rat race anymore; they come out of university saying, 'I don't want to work for anyone. I want to be my own boss'. A good proportion of those already on the corporate ladder can't wait to jump off and start a business so that they too can escape.

The thing is, becoming an entrepreneur isn't about avoiding the discipline of a nine-to-five job or jumping into the next "it" industry because other people seem to be making money. Becoming an entrepreneur is about finding a problem that you are uniquely placed to solve and that people will pay you for. You shouldn't be thinking about a "me too", copy and paste approach because the idea of working for yourself sounds appealing. The thought process should be, *what skills or resources do I have to execute that idea? Am I passionate enough about it to pursue it and follow through?*

3.   *The myth that good ideas are the key to business success*

We live in a world where the future of success is touted as becoming an entrepreneur, so the focus of most graduates is to be the next Elon Musk or Sara Blakely and create the next Tesla or Spanx. The thought around this is powerful, but it is not the full story. Ideas are a dime a dozen;

execution and the ability to solve a series of problems is the actual key to success.

Becoming an entrepreneur means you are responsible for an enterprise and beyond the idea—a successful enterprise has to have structure, a business model and a value proposition. Instead of over-glamorising either end of the spectrum, let's focus on encouraging people to be value-driven. solve problems where they are and focus on finding career paths that suit their skill-set and temperament so they can thrive.

EXERCISE: DISCOVER YOUR PURPOSE

1. Write down at least three skills that can improve your earning potential.
2. In your everyday job (even if you hate your job) what particular tasks do you do well? For example, you are an analyst; do you hate research but you like building business models?
3. What problems do your friends call you to solve?
4. What are ten things can you do every day to improve your mastery in these skills? For example, research courses, find a mentor, understudy someone who does what you want to do, taking out two hours a day to perfect or practice.
5. Write down ten things you complain about every day.
6. Break the problems down into smaller tasks.
7. What skills do you have that can solve a specific aspect of the problem?
8. How can you package your skill set to create value that people will pay you for?
9. What five things are you uniquely placed to do?

CHAPTER 12:
BECOMING A SMART MONEY WOMAN

Zuri looked on in amusement as Tsola rummaged in the closet. "What are you doing, getting ready to go play squash again?"

"Yeah. That dinner at Sevruga was great but I don't want to pack on the pounds so I have to stay active," Tsola responded.

Zuri took in his trim, fit frame and laughed. "You are *so* vain."

"Vain, *ke*? You don't want me to lose this six-pack do you?" He joked back. "What are your plans this morning? Spa? Beach? Because I know you have no plans to work out this holiday," he quipped.

"Leave me alone, *jo*," she said and playfully tossed a pillow at him. "I plan to do just that and in that exact order as well. Sue me!"

"No need to get violent young lady! Let's meet for lunch at Nobu at one. I'm having coffee and a quick meeting with Matt after I beat him at squash."

"Sounds great! But I thought you weren't working on this holiday Mr. Preware?" Zuri couldn't resist teasing him. Tsola was such a workaholic and didn't do downtime very well.

"This money isn't going to make itself, babe," he replied with a grin as he shut the door behind him.

Zuri headed to the balcony with her money journal in hand to work on tracking her progress for the month. It gave order to what could have been the chaos of her financial life because every month she could give herself a monthly performance review tracking her income, expenses, goals and, it kept her accountable. It was still her favourite gift from Tsola, because it was thoughtful and really had made the most impact in her life.

Done, she leaned on the railing and looked at the picturesque view of Table Mountain from her balcony suite as a slight breeze drifted through her hair. They were staying at the One and Only resort in Cape Town and Tsola had really gone all out planning this holiday. He had booked a lush two-bedroom suite and it had been a series of dinners, spa treatments, and meeting up for drinks with Tsola's business associates in South Africa.

Their relationship had come a long way in recent months, and it felt like they had a better understanding of each other. He had introduced her to new music, new books and a different perspective on life. Despite his incredibly busy schedule, Tsola still found ways for them to have fun and enjoy their relationship and she never felt neglected. In fact, she loved that he was so focused and she truly admired his passion for his work. The man thought no small thoughts, it was always go big or go home—in everything that he did. Even with her, Tsola made it clear that he wanted to see her win so he was investing his time, supporting her dreams, challenging her, and she would even go as far as to say, inspiring her creativity. His ambition and the vision that he had for his own life could be intimidating; she knew Tsola couldn't be with a woman who wasn't driven. At first that scared her, but in the last four months her drive was at the max.

The last twelve months had been a struggle for the people she cared about, but for better or worse they had all come out stronger. Her mother had settled back into the family home and was still calling every week to harass her about getting married. Tami, Lara, Ladun and Adesuwa had all been through different degrees of changes but their bond remained just as powerful. And with things with Tsola looking promising, for the first time in a long time she was excited about her future.

Life was good at work, too. She had become a superstar at Richmond and her idea to build the new division had panned out, now contributing around three percent to the company's bottom line—but her success had not come without a few teething problems.

At first it had been difficult to get more than ten interior designers to sign up and pay to be on the platform and they needed a critical mass for it succeed. Only the designers she had worked with in the past were willing to participate, and Mr. Tunde had started to get jittery half way into the second month because it seemed like there was no traction and the firm was unwilling to spend any more money on marketing. So she had gotten creative and decided that the only way to get buy-in was to show them just what the platform could do.

She'd had a light bulb moment and decided to use social media to display the work of the interior designers who had worked with Richmond in the past and had managed to expand their clientele as well as improve their profit margins. The substantial revenues they were raking in were sizeable in comparison to the nominal fee plus commission they had to pay to be on the platform.

She showcased the value the platform was bringing to the clients that were keen to publicly endorse the service; people who had specific tastes but didn't want the hassle of trying furniture shopping in Nigeria to hunt down the perfect piece for their homes. Even the furniture stores were enjoying the extra traffic the platform was bringing, along with the increased sales.

By month three, not only had Mr Tunde promoted her to a junior vice president, the role had come with a salary bump even more than the twenty percent increase she had originally asked for. This was thanks to the members of the board who were all duly impressed by her initiative in building an entirely new revenue stream for the company.

On occasion she still felt like an imposter, that she didn't deserve the success, but she also knew it was self-doubt raising its ugly head.

She wasn't a billionaire, but she felt like she was more in control of her money and she had started investing towards her goal of building assets in stocks and land. Instead of giving in to instant gratification and impulsive spending, she chose to spend her money intentionally on purchases that supported her goals, which could sometimes mean the Chloé Drew bag she had been lusting over. As a matter of fact, these days, such an expensive splurge was usually a reward for reaching a long-term financial goal. She had successfully created systems around her money that allowed her to prioritise her goals, live well, and make better choices.

Zuri was learning to own where she was in her journey and stay true to her authentic self. She felt like she was no longer on a career ladder to nowhere and though she hadn't quite figured out her purpose, she felt she was on her way there. She finally understood that building wealth was about creating more options for herself long-term. And, she was starting to realise that if she stayed rooted in trying to discover said purpose and the contribution she was born to make in this world, doors would open for her. Zuri had discovered she was her own hero.

SMART MONEY LESSON: THE DEFINITION OF A SMART MONEY WOMAN

The Smart Money Woman—she is the woman we should all aspire to be, financially!

She is a combination of the best parts of African women I respect. She has an entrepreneurial mind and sits on several boards like Ibukun Awosika. She is a pioneer of industry and creates jobs like Tara Fela Durotoye and Yewande Zacchaeus. She is fearless like Mo Abudu, who had the guts to pursue a dream of owning her own network regardless of how impossible it seemed. She is committed to raising the next generation of female leaders like Osayi Alile. She shapes the narrative of new African culture like Bolanle Austen-Peters. And, she has the financial mind of women like Nimi Akinkugbe, Arunma Oteh and Bola Adesola.

She is a woman whose hustle has purpose and has learnt to make money, keep money and grow money. She is a master of her craft, lives by her own playbook, and is in the top ten percent of her industry.

She doesn't worry about whether there's money in the new fad industry. She has found her calling in life, something that matches her passion with her skill set and, regardless of where she is in that process, she is excited and confident that she will make money because she has positioned herself for success and she knows this is where she can maximise her earning potential.

Ultimately, improving her net worth is more important than upgrading her wardrobe. This mind set helps her reason when she's spending. Buying a designer bag becomes a reward for reaching a long-term financial goal as opposed to buying one just because there's money in her account. She derives the same amount of joy from investing in assets as she does spending on her lifestyle expenses. She would rather live like a princess forever than live like a queen for a few years.

She is the sort of woman that we are all capable of becoming. I've described who she is to me, but I want every woman who reads this book create and become her own version of the Smart Money Woman.

Printed in Great Britain
by Amazon